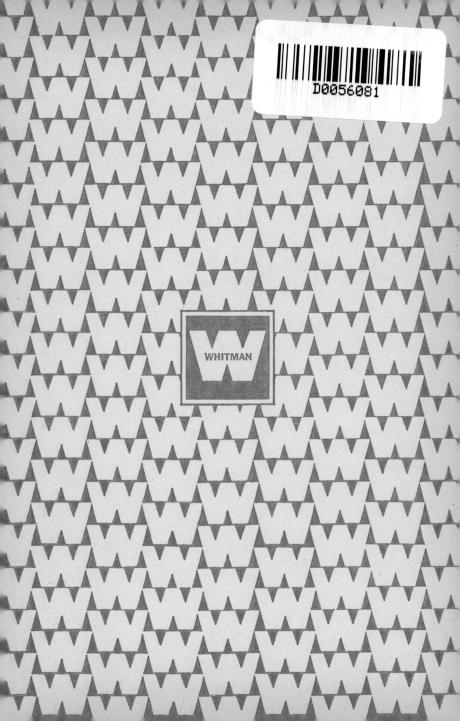

MYSTERY AND DANGER!

Explosive tension ... brutal body contact ... punishing fast action—these were all accepted and expected as part of the rough, tough game of professional ice hockey. What Bud Carson didn't expect—and didn't deserve—was the added burden of playing under a cloud of suspicion from teammates and fans.

When Bud's father, player-coach of the Boise Battlers, died in an apparent car accident, a paper bag full of cash was found beside his body. Rumors started: The money was a payoff for "fixing" a game. His father's guilt was never proved, but now, a year later, suspicion has fallen on Bud, outstanding young captain of the same Boise Battlers.

Bud Carson must clear his father's name and his own ... must discover which of his teammates is deliberately causing Battler losses ... must find out if gambling interests are involved. In searching for answers, Bud uncovers something else: Murder has been committed! Time is running out as the killer casts a heavy SHADOW ON THE ICE.

SHADOW on the ICE

by Carl Henry Rathjen

illustrated by Ben Otero

®A WHITMAN BOOK
Western Publishing Company, Inc.
Racine, Wisconsin

CONTENTS

1
Shoot the Puck!

T<small>EN</small> . . . <small>NINE</small> . . . <small>EIGHT</small>. . . ."

Hockey fans counted the final seconds in the Can-Am Hockey League game. The visiting Canadian team, the Regina Regals, had the professional minor league game locked up at 3–2 and intended to keep it that way until the buzzer sounded.

Idaho fans screamed urgently as their hometown six, the Boise Battlers, took the puck down the rink, their last desperate attempt to tie the score and save themselves from a loss.

Bud Carson, right wingman of the Battlers, raced along the boards, watching the puck being stickhandled up the far side of the ice. Beside him, the orange-jerseyed Regal defenseman closed in, seeking to pocket him against the boards. Bud skated faster.

The Regal player pushed to keep pace with Bud. Suddenly Bud gouged ice, slowing just enough to let the defender slip ahead. Bud surged behind him and out from the boards.

The puck zipped across the rink from Art Schoen, purple-jerseyed left wingman. It was too long a pass—nearly intercepted by the Regal covering the Battler center. But Bud's extended stick scooped it in and took it over the blue line and into the attack zone.

No buzzer yet, ending the game. So maybe. . . .

Behind Bud, the defenseman's blades rang as he desperately tried to close in and check. Ahead, all was clear. The heavily padded Regal goalie crouched in the goal crease, eyes gleaming behind his face mask. The goalie didn't move; he was not going to be deked—decoyed into a premature defense action—until the puck was on its way.

Bud felt a flash of indecision. Should he try a

slap shot in spite of the goalie's alertness? At the last instant, he swerved left in front of the crease, too far out for the goalie's stick to poke check the puck.

Bud backhanded the puck toward Lou Huff, the Battler center, coming up the slot between the red face-off circles. Lou would have a clear shot at the goal, with Bud's body screening him from the goalie's view. Lou drove forward, but not fast enough. The puck skimmed past his reaching stick and skittered to the side boards as the final buzzer sounded.

Regina over Boise, 3–2.

The victorious cheers of Canadian rooters were drowned out by the dismayed groans of the Boise fans. It was an angry dismay, laced with boos and catcalls. Bud caught stinging words.

"Can-it Carson!" "Game-thrower!" "Just like his old man!"

Bud felt his insides knot. Maybe he himself should have tried for the goal. Yet if he'd failed, the reaction of the fans would probably have been exactly the same.

The fans still had their doubts about the Battlers. Bud's father, Bart Carson, had been player-coach of the team until his death last season. He'd been in an auto accident after the team had lost a very important game—and a large sum of money was found in his wrecked car.

Ugly rumors developed, rumors that Bart Carson was being paid to throw key games. A thorough investigation followed, but nothing was proved—or disproved. The rumors persisted, despite Bud's efforts to clear his father's name.

A Regal player swirled by. "Tough luck," he said, grinning.

"Yeah," Bud grunted.

Boos and catcalls still echoed from the stands. Bud wondered if he would keep on hearing them no matter where he went, whatever team he played with. The Battlers had trusted his father; they trusted him. Or did they?

He glanced toward Art Schoen and other players from the bench as they skated toward the dressing room. Were they thinking that he had deliberately thrown away the puck?

Lou Huff glided by, touched Bud's arm. "Sorry," he murmured.

Sorry for what? Bud wondered. Was Lou apologizing because he'd been too slow to get that pass? Or was he sorry that Bud had placed it beyond reach?

Bud realized that voicing any such questions would only arouse resentment. Ignoring the taunts from angry fans still in the stands, he skated slowly off the rink.

At the edge of the rink, Bob Dupuis, right defenseman for the Battlers, waved his stick at a vehement spectator and threatened to climb into the stands. Bud had to grin. The big French Canadian, built like a blacksmith, had been almost lost among too many other hockey candidates in his home province. He had been discovered by Bart Carson and brought south of the border to play with the Battlers. He had regarded Bart Carson almost as a father, and he thought of Bud as a brother.

Bud grasped Dupuis's arm as he began to hoist himself over the boards. "Lay off that, Peewee."

Dupuis's eyes were hot coals. "*Sacre-bleu!* If you won't get mad, then somebody's got to do it for you!"

"I *am* mad," Bud declared, pulling him away from the stands. "But anger alone isn't going to stop what people are beginning to think."

"*Oui,*" Dupuis agreed reluctantly, glowering as they walked on their skates along the rubber mat toward the dressing room. "But what else can we do when we can't prove anything?"

"Nothing, so far," Bud admitted. "We'll just have to keep trying to find some way to clear Dad's name."

"And *yours,* too," Dupuis added.

Bud nodded resignedly. "I guess I looked pretty bad to the fans tonight."

Dupuis snorted. "I could name some others who—"

"No," Bud interrupted firmly. "We've got a good team this season. Let's not mess it up with wild accusations."

Dupuis shrugged, muttering to himself.

Bud saw Al Tierney, head coach, waiting outside the dressing room door. Al had played in the big leagues with Bud's father until age had slowed them both down. He'd been coaching another farm team in the minor league at the time of Bart Carson's death and had been summoned to the Battlers. His strong, bony face, scarred by sticks and skates, wore neither frown nor smile as he looked at Bud.

"Gleason wants to see you. But step into the dressing room for a moment first."

Gleason was the club owner. Did he have suspicions, too? Bud wondered, following Dupuis and Tierney into the dressing room. The coach closed the door. Thick silence filled the room; Tierney never had to raise his voice to get attention.

"I don't like to rub your noses in defeat," Tierney snapped, "but while it's fresh in your minds, let's look at your mistakes, working back from what just happened."

He stabbed a finger toward Art Schoen, left wingman, who had zipped the puck to Bud. His voice also stabbed.

"Brilliant! *Real* brilliant! Clear across the ice! A beautiful way to lose possession!"

Art Schoen protested to the coach. "I saw Bud coming clear toward—"

"No alibis!" Tierney cut in. "A short pass to the point would have been more logical and safer for Lou to set up a play."

Tierney turned to Bud.

"So he was lucky and got it to you. And then you—"

"I had two options," Bud admitted, "but I thought Lou had a better—"

"When in doubt, always shoot for the goal." Without pausing, the coach went on to Lou Huff. "And why in blazes weren't you up there to get the puck when Bud passed it?"

Dupuis nudged Bud. Lou Huff hesitated, then shrugged. "You said you didn't want alibis."

Tierney's glance flicked to Bud. "I'll talk to you again later. Gleason's waiting."

Bud unlaced his shoes. As he handed his skates to Dupuis, the defenseman murmured, *"Jette le palet."*

Shoot the puck. Bud pretended not to hear Dupuis's plea to defend himself, if necessary, by tossing suspicions about teammates.

The rubber mat and then the unprotected floor felt cold under his sweaty socks as Bud went toward the office of Tex Gleason, manager and major owner of the Battlers.

Gleason had been a rancher in Texas until oil was discovered on his spread, whereupon he sold off his cattle and went into various sports. He didn't have the ability to participate, but he had the money to back those who did. He started with racehorses, then financed the construction of racing cars. He owned, just briefly, a minor league ball team, but baseball was too slow to suit him. Next he went into basketball, but he came to feel that the scoring was too easy and, therefore, excessive.

Then, on a trip to Canada, he discovered the rough and fast game of ice hockey. He also met Bart Carson, who was getting a little too slow for National Hockey League play. Together, they got an NHL franchise to build a Can-Am minor league team as a farm for the New York Rangers. While Gleason built a rink in Boise, Idaho, Bart Carson scouted college and semipro teams, north and south of the border, to get players for the Battler club.

In their first season, the Battlers surprised everyone by winning third place in the Can-Am League play-offs. A couple of their best players were summoned to the Ranger bench, but several strong youngsters moved in to help fill the gap. The team continued to grow and began to attract more and more attention.

Then, during the previous season, strange things began happening. The Battlers won a few games the odds-makers had called impossible. They also lost several games to teams of half their strength.

Bud's father had seemed unusually nervous on the night of their critical play-off game. Immediately afterward, while the Battlers were still stunned by their unexpected loss, he disappeared.

Bart Carson was found in his wrecked car the following morning. Underneath his coat was a paper sack filled with money. Talk was quick to start . . . that he'd been paid for throwing the play-off game—and probably other games before that.

Now, after tonight's last-minute loss, those who were always ready to think the worst were doing it: Like father, like son.

Taking a deep breath, Bud knocked at the office door, then opened it. Deep-pile carpeting, squirming under his socks, proclaimed the Battler colors, purple and gold. The drapes at a broad window looking out onto a downtown Boise street were gold with purple trim. A large desk held a telephone, a bucking bronco statuette, a goldplated puck, and Tex Gleason's feet, in tooled-leather cowmen's boots.

The club owner's gray eyes regarded Bud over the tips of the boots. A spotless, cream-colored Stetson clung to the back of his balding head. His gaze never left Bud as he reached out to draw the drapes when a couple of irate fans outside spotted Bud and began to shout.

"I expected you to come in with a bloodied head," he remarked.

"It's still a good possibility," Bud admitted.

Gleason nodded. "I hear our fans lost a lot of dough tonight."

"Too bad," Bud murmured, then added, "and now some of them are thinking that I made some."

Gleason said nothing.

Bud paused, while those gray eyes just looked steadily at him. "Tex . . . Mr. Gleason . . . do you think that I—"

The gray eyes sharpened. "Should I?"

"No!" Bud snapped.

"If you don't want annoying questions," Gleason said mildly, "then stop trying to put suspicions in my mind. Sit down." He gestured toward a plate of sectioned oranges on a side table. Hockey players had found them to be better than water for quenching thirst. Bud shook his head and sat down, facing the club owner.

"All right, Bud, I'm listening. What about those final seconds?"

Bud shrugged. "We had a chance to tie the game, and I blew it."

"I saw." Gleason motioned toward a closed-circuit TV. "You say *you* blew it. Why?"

Bud explained about his split-second decision

to pass the puck to Lou Huff. He blamed himself for shooting it too far in advance of the center.

"I thought you led it just right for him, Bud," Gleason said.

There was something behind that observation, and Bud wasn't sure he liked what it was. For a long moment there was just silence. Then Gleason scowled.

"Come on, Bud, speak up. I want to get to the bottom of all this." He lowered his boots from the desk. "Do you think Lou deliberately missed your pass?"

Bud recalled Dupuis's murmured *jette le palet*. Well, why not? It would be an easy way to get off the hook, tossing suspicion at Lou. Never mind that it might have been only that Lou was tired from the hard, fast game. Let Lou do some sweating and feel the frustrated anger over unwarranted accusations. . . .

"No," Bud said more to himself than to Gleason. Then he spoke decidedly. "I won't say anything like that about Lou."

Gleason leaned forward. "What about Art Schoen's long pass? Could he have been expecting it to be intercepted?"

"He got it to me," Bud reminded him.

"What about earlier in the game," Gleason persisted, "when we lost our two-to-one lead?"

Bud gestured toward the TV. "You saw the action better than I could on the ice."

Gleason smiled slightly. "Don't tell the paying customers that." He became serious again. "You know what I'm trying to pin down. In order to fix a game, there has to be somebody doing it on the ice."

"I agree with that." Then Bud shook his head. "But too many things can happen to make a guy look bad. An opposing forward may make a good forecheck against a defenseman. That happened to Peewee in the second period, and I sure wouldn't suspect *him* of being involved in fixing. I got a rough shoulder check at the start of the third period. Peewee dug out the puck from the Regal forward almost immediately and shot it back to me, because Lou wasn't clear. I was still dazed from crashing into the boards, and I didn't catch the puck." Bud shook his head again. "You can look at any action from the wrong point of view."

Gleason was silent for a moment. "In other words, you're not willing to point a finger at anyone, even if I am."

"I don't know of anything to justify doing that." Bud frowned. "It's your right as owner and manager, but unless you've got something concrete. . . ."

"Well?"

"It's obvious, isn't it?" Bud said. "If all you have is a suspicion, with nothing solid to back it up, you'd only be hurting the team—and yourself."

"*You're* the one I'm trying to protect," the owner declared.

"Thanks for the vote of confidence," Bud said.

Gleason waved that aside. "Don't put a halo on me. I've got a wallet I'm thinking of, too. You're more than just Bart's son to me. You're the guts of our first attack line. The club needs you. So we've *got* to find some way to take the heat off you and put it where it belongs."

"I sure wouldn't mind that," Bud admitted. "It's easy to act as though the boos don't bother you, but inside, they do. I'm sure glad Dad wasn't getting them while he was alive."

Gleason nodded. "But he suspected something before he died. Can you recall anything specific he might have said to you?"

"I've been wracking my brain ever since he

died." Bud fell silent, thinking back again. For years, ice hockey, in contrast to many other pro sports, had remained reasonably free of scandal. But with the expansion of the leagues, there were more clubs, more players, and more money involved. There were bound to be some people who would be ready to capitalize on it.

Bud and his father had realized that all games couldn't be won. But in the previous season, they began to wonder when key games went down the drain for no obvious reason . . . games in which there was a lot of money riding on the Battlers . . . games in which the odds all favored the Battlers. Gleason began to hear rumors from his contacts off the rink, and Bart Carson had sought the pipeline into the club.

"I'm positive," Bud sighed, "that Dad was getting close to something. But, just like me now, he wasn't sure enough to talk about it." Bud leaned forward, placing his fist on the desk. "I think he pinned it on someone that night, in the last game he played."

Gleason grimaced. "I've run and rerun the tapes of that game. So have you. I've talked to the other players. So have you."

"Dad spotted something," Bud insisted, "something that made him sure, got him close." Bud stood up, now thumping the desk with his fist. "That's why he was killed. He got too close. I don't care what the police reports said about his automobile 'accident.' I think he was murdered and that money planted on him to divert suspicion from someone else." Bud's fist pounded harder. "And if it takes me the rest of my life, I'm going to find out who—"

"I'm with you," Gleason interrupted. "I go along with you that he was framed to divert attention from someone else, so there would be opportunity to fix games again. Maybe it started up again tonight. Maybe not." Gleason stood up, leaning over the desk toward Bud. "But I won't go along with your making the same mistake your father made—keeping things to himself. I want your promise that you'll tell me anything you might find out. Anything!"

Bud frowned. "As I said, I hate to point a finger on just suspicion, without anything solid to—"

"All right," Gleason agreed. "But if it's a *strong* suspicion, I want to know about it. Maybe it will fit with something from my end. It's our only chance, Bud. We've got to make this a team play. Just remember your father. This is something too big and dangerous for one man."

"Okay," Bud conceded.

They shook hands and walked to the door together.

"Be careful," Gleason warned, and then he smiled. "Except when you're on the ice and we've got a game to win."

As Bud left the office, the dressing room door just down the corridor was closing quietly. Bud suddenly had the feeling that someone had been eavesdropping outside the office. He hurried toward the dressing room. If he could just find out who. . . .

2
Off-Balance

BEFORE BUD COULD REACH the dressing room door, it opened again. The man who stepped out was Sid Seidler, roving sportswriter. With his sparse sandy hair, octagonal-rimmed glasses, tweed jacket, and sport shirt, he looked huskier than he really was. What he lacked in muscle he made up for with punch in his writing. He had once called the rough, bloody game of pro ice hockey "legalized assault and battery."

"Bud!" he exclaimed. "Just the man I'm looking for. What about tonight's game? Make it fit to print, whatever you're thinking!"

Bud shrugged. "You can't win 'em all. Sid, I'm looking for someone, too. Who just went into the dressing room?"

Sid's sandy eyebrows came together thoughtfully above the rims of the glasses. "I didn't see—"

"You just came out," Bud declared. "You must have—"

"I stepped into the washroom after garnering the game postmortems. There was no one coming in this door as I came out. I must have just missed seeing him."

The slam of a locker door could be heard in the corridor. Sid smiled. "That was probably Peewee. Or maybe the chip falling off his shoulder." Seidler studied Bud. "Have you got any further comments about tonight?"

Bud shook his head, then spoke carefully. "And what are you going to write about it?"

Sid pursed his lips. "I guess I'll say it was a well-played game. Very decorous, for a change— on the ice, that is. Very gentlemanly. No dirty tactics, no bloody heads. But I can't say that all of the paying customers were happy. Hockey fans can create their own mayhem if they don't see what they want on the ice."

Bud didn't know what to say to that. He didn't want to get into a discussion of the boos and accusations that had been hurled at him.

"See you around," he said and entered the dressing room. The air was gloomy and thick with the smell of liniment and sweat, damp with steam from the showers. Bud glanced about, trying to surmise who might have just entered the room a few minutes ago. Some of the players were just going to or coming from the showers. Others were half-dressed. A few still dawdled in their hockey gear. Chuck Ainsworth, the Battlers' number one goalie, was dressed for the street and approaching the door. He still had a black eye from a week ago when a slap shot had struck his face mask. He seemed to be in a hurry to get out, nodding his blond head curtly and reaching for the door.

Bud grasped his arm. "You made some nice saves tonight, Chuck."

"Thanks." He shoved on out of the dressing room. Bud wondered, glancing after him. Rod Stevens, left defense, known as "Ramrod" for the way he could tumble an offense to the ice, also came hurrying from farther back in the locker room, rushing to catch up with the goalie.

"What's with Chuck?" Bud asked.

"His old man's in the hospital again," Rod answered without breaking stride. "Chuck's told him not to come to games. Too much excitement." Rod gained the corridor and shouted, "Chuck, wait for me."

Bud frowned. Chuck had been with the club last year and had had a lot of medical expenses for his father and other members of his family. Would that make him vulnerable to whoever might want to fix games?

Bud went farther into the dressing room. Peewee Dupuis was winding new black tape on his stick blade.

"Did you see who came in just a few moments ahead of me?" Bud asked.

Dupuis shook his head. "What did you tell Tex?"

"Later," Bud murmured as he saw Al Tierney crossing the room.

"Practice tomorrow morning," Tierney said curtly. "Nine o'clock."

"Wait a minute!" Bud objected. "It's Saturday. Peewee and I have a kids' team we're coaching at nine."

"This outfit needs some coaching, too," Tierney retorted. Before he could be reminded that the rink was leased for other activities besides pro hockey, he went on. "All right, we'll make it *six* A.M." He turned and raised his voice as he addressed the rest of the players. "Six A.M. sharp!"

Voices rose in protest as Tierney walked out of the dressing room. Dupuis stared at the closing door, then rolled his dark gaze up to Bud.

"He knew," he muttered. "Always it is Saturday for the bantams." Dupuis's black eyebrows rose. "Maybe, Bud, he does not want us to have time to forget tonight."

Bud glanced at the Battlers remaining in the dressing room. No one seemed to be blaming him for an early practice. He pulled off his purple jersey and sat on the bench as he removed the protective pads.

"While I was with Gleason, were there any cracks about me?"

"No. Just that it was another game. We lost it. We do better next week against Calgary."

"That shouldn't be too much trouble," Bud agreed. "The Oilers have been hurt by injuries. But the way things have been going for us—" He stopped, then frowned. "You know, Peewee, that's the funny part."

"*Qu'est-ce que c'est?*" Dupuis asked.

"That we lose when it's least expected," Bud explained. "We did that when Dad was alive, too, last season."

Dupuis nodded. "We win some games. We forget to remain watchful for when we lose one. We are deked."

"No more," Bud declared. "Every game from now on is *it*."

"*Oui*." Dupuis examined the new taping, then hefted his stick. "And if we find someone responsible, he will feel this."

"But only if there's good reason," Bud cautioned. "We can't go swinging wild just on suspicion. Tex concedes that, too."

Dupuis patted the hockey stick. "We will find good reason."

"Come on," said Bud. "Let's get home and get some sleep. We've got to get up early."

Home was Bud's sister's place east of Boise. As they drove out Warm Springs Avenue, Bud glanced up at the lighted cross on Table Rock. Bart Carson's car had hurtled down the precipice from up there. Rumor had it that he'd probably gone there for the payoff for throwing the game. It had been snowing that night; the roads were bad. Bud's hands tightened angrily on the wheel. Beside him, Dupuis, who had also been looking up, nodded.

"Anger is like the sugar in grapes, *mon ami*. It ferments the wine, but we must not let it become vinegar."

Bud grinned. "That's funny coming from you. You want to suspect everybody within reach."

"It puzzles me, too," said Dupuis.

They were laughing when they arrived home.

At six the next morning, the club was suited up and on the ice. Chuck Ainsworth looked as though he had two black eyes, from being up all night, waiting for word about his father in intensive care.

Al Tierney blew his whistle.

They skated in pairs along the boards and around behind the nets. A second sharp blast from the whistle, and they skated faster. Two whistle blasts, and all skated backward, a drill that was especially important for defensemen, so they could keep their eyes on action up the rink.

Next, Tierney put the club through figure eights, barking at some members who, like most skaters, were better at turning to the left than to the right.

After half an hour of hard skating drill, Tierney gestured toward the target board hung on the far goal, then skidded a box of pucks in front of Bud.

"Slap shots and backhands," he called to another player. "Feed Bud the pucks, and let *him* retrieve the rebounds."

Bud skated in from the boards, just as he had last night, receiving the pucks and shooting them for the scant inches of air to either side of the board hanging before the net. Meanwhile, Lou Huff was getting extra exercise for missing that pass last night.

"Lou," Tierney ordered, "down the sideboards. Dupuis, meet him. Back-check."

Dupuis smiled at Lou.

Later, Tierney sent the attack line—Bud, Lou Huff, and Art Schoen—around and around the rink with a puck, practicing short passes while they skated fast. Art to Lou, Lou to Bud, back to Lou from Bud, then to Art.

"Break up that pattern!" Tierney barked.

Then there were barrages of pucks fired at the goalies, by one player after another, to give defensive practice, too. When nine o'clock came, the club was sweating as though they had played three sudden-death overtime periods.

Art Schoen muttered to Bud, "He's sure sore about last night."

Bud didn't know how to answer that. Was Art Schoen referring specifically to his mistake?

Later, Bud mentioned that to Dupuis as they chewed oranges and let the juice trickle down their throats.

Dupuis shrugged. "Maybe Tierney is covering up for himself. It is possible, even for a coach. He did have the second line on the ice last night when we lost the lead."

"Yeah." Bud frowned. "Not for long, but just long enough. . . ." He shook his head. "But Tierney wasn't even with us last season when Dad was alive."

"*Oui.* But didn't we lose some games against his weaker Pirates?"

"You and your suspicions!" Bud sighed.

"I have a new one," Dupuis murmured, nodding toward the end of the rink. The first of the bantams, young Mark Strickland, had arrived.

He must have suited up at home, including his skates. He was removing the guards from the blades while his mother and father hurriedly approached Bud through the lower tier of stands. "I have the suspicion," Dupuis murmured, "that *Papa* and *Maman* Push are going to do some more pushing."

"You don't have to *suspect* that," Bud muttered. Bantam ice hockey, like Little League baseball, had its share of parents who *knew* they had better judgment than the coaches.

"Good morning," Bud greeted the Stricklands.

"Hi, Bud," replied Wayne Strickland. A computer operator in a large Northwest banking organization, he sported a moustache that was much too thick for his lean face. "You're in for a real surprise this morning," he said, nodding toward Mark, who was skating down the rink.

Willowy Mrs. Strickland's hair always made Bud wonder what brand of brass polish she used. She let him have the full benefit of her smile. "We're sure you'll want Mark to be your number one forward."

"Every boy on the squad," Bud answered carefully, "is positioned and played according to his ability."

"That's just the point," Wayne Strickland said with a smile. "Wait'll you see how Mark's shooting has improved. Watch this!" He grabbed a puck from the supply box and scaled it along the ice toward his son. "Mark—sock it home!"

The bantam's skates shaved ice as he came to a stop. He positioned his hockey stick, caught the skidding puck, and slammed it into the net, twenty feet away.

"Again," Strickland yelled, sliding another puck across the rink.

Mark's skates chopped the ice to intercept it. He stopped the puck with his stick, planted his skates, and hit the net again.

"How's that for an angle shot?" Strickland asked Bud.

"Hasn't he improved marvelously?" Mrs. Strickland twittered. "You needn't have any hesitation now about—"

"I built him a goal in the backyard," her husband cut in, "and every day, before and after school—"

Bud nodded. "That's what it takes to make a hockey player: constant practice." He moved out onto the ice to avoid further prompting from the Stricklands. "Nice shooting, Mark. But now let's do it without coming to a stop. In hockey, you've got to keep skating." He fed a few pucks to Mark in front of the net and to the side. "Don't stop, Mark. Keep skating while you shoot."

The boy tried but was no longer the marksman, getting himself awkwardly off-balance and shooting with his weight on the wrong foot, so that his body wasn't behind the shot.

Later, when Bud and Dupuis were drilling the club of youngsters, they continually spotted Mark gliding through his turns instead of skating them. On one swing around the nets, when he tried to skate instead of coast, his feet tangled and he went down, spilling a couple of other bantams.

In play, Bud gave him a chance at forward, to pacify his frowning parents, watching from the stands. Mark couldn't get the puck near the goal unless he maintained his balance by gliding or coming to a complete stop.

When the bantam session was over, Dupuis frowned beside Bud. "I do not like what I see. I do not mean *le garçon*. Mark tried, but his *papa* and *maman* are angry and disappointed."

Bud nodded. "I'll see if I can choke it off." He overtook Mark, who was disconsolately dragging his stick toward his angrily waiting parents. Bud's

glove patted Mark's helmet, a required piece of gear in this league. "Mark," he said, loudly enough for the Stricklands to overhear, "I've got a suggestion for improving your skating. Then, with that marksmanship, you may very well become a first-class forward."

Mark's freckled face brightened as he looked up at Bud. "What's that, Mr. Carson?"

"It'll be up to your parents, if they're willing to help you."

The Stricklands shifted their eyes from Mark to Bud. "He needs something," Wayne Strickland growled.

"His performance this morning was very disappointing," Mrs. Strickland complained. Her distraught gaze flicked to Mark, then back to Bud. "I don't understand. You said his improvement depended on us. We've made sure that he has the very best gear—"

Bud nodded, placing his hand reasuringly on Mark's shoulder. "What Mark really needs is some coaching in his skating. He's got to have his skates under control and keep his balance at all times. He could probably be a natural hockey player if he lived in Canada. Kids up there have more opportunity to become skilled skaters."

Wayne Strickland scowled. "Beth and I try to get him to the rink as often as possible."

"That's good, but it's not enough. He needs some professional coaching to improve his ability on skates. If you'll go along with what I suggest, I'm positive his improvement will be very rapid."

Now he had their interest and attention. "Okay," said Wayne Strickland, and his wife nodded. "What do you suggest?"

"Enroll Mark in a figure skating class."

Mark pulled away indignantly from Bud. "That's for girls!"

"For men, too," Bud said. "Haven't you attended ice shows or seen the Olympics on TV?"

"But I don't want to be a figure skater. I want to play hockey." Mark's freckles bunched together indignantly. "Who ever heard of a tough hockey player—"

"Don't say it," Bud cut in. "You'll be wrong. I know of one NHL coach who sent two of his players to figure skating class to learn better control on skates."

"*Oui,*" said Dupuis, who had been listening in. "Just like this."

He launched out onto the ice and flowed around in a graceful arch, on one foot, thick arms gently extended, and pudgy fingers waving daintily.

"You look like a dancing gorilla!" Bud called, but he nodded approvingly at Peewee.

The rink organist had arrived, and suddenly the arena was filled with a lilting waltz in rhythm with Dupuis's figures. The bantams and their parents laughed and cheered.

Peewee hammed it up. Sweeping by the side of the rink, he snatched his hockey stick and pretended it was a skating partner. Then, as he skated, pirouetting and cutting standard figures in the ice, he swung the stick in slap and flip shot motions. Bud scooted a puck out to him. Still figure skating with surprising grace, forward and backward, spinning and swirling, Dupuis skillfully stickhandled the puck around and around the rink.

Bud glanced at Mark. "Well?"

Mark turned eagerly to his parents. "Can I?"

"*May* I," his mother corrected him.

Wayne Strickland nodded.

In the dressing room, Bud grinned at Dupuis as they changed into street clothes. "Thanks. If you ever give up hockey, you can try out for the chorus line of the Ice Follies."

Dupuis chuckled. "Well, we pushed *Papa* and *Maman* Push off our necks for a little while, anyway."

"I didn't suggest it for that reason," Bud said. "I really think Mark could be a terrific forward if he were a better skater."

"He will learn," said Dupuis. "I saw the fire in his eyes." Peewee sighed. "Now if we could direct our suspicions just as easily—"

"That's no problem," Bud said. "It's easy to suspect. The tough part is finding some hard evidence to back it up."

"*Oui,*" Dupuis agreed. "And speaking of evidence, I learned why Tierney made us sweat this morning. Not just because of last night. The Oilers' injuries are not as bad as we heard. They'll have full strength on the ice when we meet them in Calgary next week."

"That's going to make it tough to spot a fixed game—if it is fixed," Bud mused. "This throws me off-balance. I was figuring that if we lost to a weaker team for no good reason. . . ."

"We play hard and we watch hard," Dupuis said. "If we see that someone on the club tries to make us lose—"

"The way I looked last night?" Bud interrupted, smiling sheepishly.

Dupuis's helpless expression said what words could not. Both men finished dressing in gloomy silence.

3
Hecklers

Bud led the Battlers out onto the ice from the dressing room. There was just a light pepper of applause, a psychological disadvantage for a visiting team playing far from home. But there were always some fans who tried to give a bit of a welcome. Bud smiled and waved his glove. Then a voice pierced out of the stands. "You won't have to throw it tonight, Carson!"

Bud's glove dropped, his hand closing into a fist. There were a few boos in the stands, directed at whoever had shouted—at least Bud hoped that was whom they were for.

Then the Oilers came out onto the ice. The arena exploded with a roar for the hometown club. Both squads began warming up.

Bud tried to dismiss the worrisome thoughts stirred up by the shout from the stands. How could that person have known about what happened in last week's game? There had been no mention of it in the Idaho paper or Sid Seidler's column. Could the shout have been arranged by an outside fixer, to keep attention away from his contact in the club?

Bud spotted Gleason's Stetson behind the Battler bench. Gleason was looking up at the stands, peering intently in the direction from which the call had originated.

When the warm-up was over, the team lineups were announced. The puck, which had been refrigerated to keep it hard, was brought out to the referee. The Battlers and Oilers skated into position around the center face-off circle.

Lou Huff, in the Battlers' gold and purple visiting jersey, won the draw when the referee dropped the puck. Using a play developed by Tierney, he shot the puck toward his own goal instead of feeding it to one of the forwards, Bud or Art Schoen. The spectators gasped.

The Oiler forwards raced toward the puck. The Battler defenseman, ready for the play, whammed it back into the neutral zone, where, clear of his surprised defenseman, Bud was ready. He stickhandled across the blue line into the attack zone. A short pass to Lou. The center drove toward the goal, then faked a pass toward Art Schoen. But his stick cleared the puck and left a drop pass for Bud, skating right behind him. Bud immediately slapped the puck into the right side of the net.

The red light flashed at 0:09 of the first period. Nine seconds of play and the Battlers led 1–0. For a moment there was stunned silence from the crowd, then some appreciative applause. Then came a thunderous roar of encouragement for the Oilers.

Again Lou Huff won the draw. He sent the puck to Art Schoen. Over the blue line again. The Oilers were aroused; the Battlers couldn't get the puck out toward the goal. Art, beseiged and in danger of losing it completely, froze the puck to the boards with his skate. The referee's whistle blew.

On the face-off in the attack zone on Art's side of the rink, the Oiler center got the draw. The Calgary five went down the rink. Dupuis and Rod Stevens skated backward, keeping themselves between the Oiler forwards and the goal. Rod hip checked his man into a sprawling crash against the boards, then raced into the corner to dig out the puck. He shot it across behind the net to Dupuis.

A poke check by the Oiler left forward failed to dislodge the puck from Dupuis. He gave Peewee a hard shoulder check into the midsection, but he bounced off the big French Canadian and fell to the ice as Peewee took the puck out and gave it to Lou Huff.

Now the Battlers went down the rink, lost the puck, and came back to save it from a goal by the Oilers. Back and forth, sticks clashing, skates ringing, the teams fought. The Battlers hung on to their lead, but the Oilers were determined to tie it and get the momentum. The action was so rapid up and down the rink that there was no opportunity for either side to make substitutions when the puck was out of its defense zone.

When the buzzer finally signaled the end of the first twenty-minute period, the score was still the same: 1–0. Bud, breathing hard as he went toward the dressing room, caught Gleason's eye. The owner nodded up toward the section of the stands from which the shout had come before the game. Gleason shook his head slightly—whatever that meant. Bud went on into the dressing room, grabbed some orange sections, and sprawled out on a bench with the rest of the Battler first team.

Tierney complimented the men on their play so far, albeit grudgingly, and ordered Remy's line, the Battlers' second line of center and forwards, to begin the second period.

"See that you keep the drive going for us," the coach added. "If it holds, we can count on the Oilers going on a rampage in the third period. That's when we'll really need our first line."

Gleason entered the locker room and moved from player to player, giving each a compliment. When he reached Bud, he lowered his voice.

"The word is that there's no big money riding on the game tonight. I tried to find out who shouted at you, but he'd left. Guess it was just one of those things."

When Bud led the club out for the second period, the same voice came from a different section of the arena. "You'd better start your swoon act, Carson!"

Bud skated to Tierney at the bench. "Put me in," he said through clenched teeth.

"You heard me," replied the coach. "Next period."

Bud waved toward the stands. "I want a chance to put a stop to that."

"What do you think you did in the first period? Forget what the poor losers say. Get on the bench."

The Remy line took the ice. Remy, the center, got the draw on the face-off. The Battler left wingman took a hip check and lost the puck. A slap shot hurtled it toward the Battler goal, and goalie Chuck Ainsworth came out of the boxed crease to meet it. Bud saw that the puck was going to hit the ice just ahead of Chuck. A bounce shot was always tricky—no telling what the puck would do. Chuck dove forward, spread-eagling himself and smothering the puck under his heavily padded body. The referee's whistle blew for a face-off in the neutral zone. He also imposed a two-minute penalty on an Oiler for slashing with his stick in an effort to keep Chuck off the puck.

The Battlers got the puck at the face-off. They

went down the rink in a power play to take advantage of the Oilers being one man short.

The Calgary fans screamed at their team's penalty killers: "Defense! Defense!"

The Oilers formed a box defense in front of the goal and refused to be penetrated.

When the two-minute penalty ended and the Oilers were back to full strength, they used it. They stormed the Battler goal. Chuck Ainsworth went down in a split to block a stinging slap shot. It rebounded from his padded leg. An Oiler lifted it in a flip shot. Chuck caught the puck in his glove and dropped it for Remy. The center took two strokes with his skates, but the puck was poke checked away from him. The attack on the Battler goal went on.

Al Tierney paced back and forth behind the Battler bench. Finally he spoke over Bud's shoulder. "Go in."

Bud tensed, knowing that his substitution could not be made until the puck was out of the defense zone. Tierney gave the word to Art Schoen and Lou Huff. It was obvious that the Remy line was faltering; Tierney knew he couldn't wait. He shouted to Remy.

The center fought desperately for possession

of the puck, and when he got it, he swung his stick like a nine iron and sent the hard rubber flying toward the far end of the rink. The linesman promptly blew his whistle. Icing the puck—sending it from the defensive end of the court all the way past the opponent's goal line, when the team was at full or equal strength—stopped play.

Bud, Lou Huff, and Art Schoen surged out from the bench.

"Nice work," Bud called to Remy. The center was too breathless to reply.

The Oilers knew that they had the momentum, and they hung on to it. At the face-off in the Battler defense zone, their center won the draw, and they retained the puck, keeping it continually on the go with short, fast passes back and forth in front of the Battler goal.

Suddenly Dupuis barged into the melee, down on one knee. He swept his stick. The puck skittered out toward Bud.

"*Allons-y!*" Peewee shouted.

"Let's go!" Bud echoed him, taking the puck out of the defense zone.

Lou Huff raced down center ice. Bud whipped the puck toward him, but the Oiler left defense got his stick on it. Bud swerved sharply to give him a hard shoulder check. As the defenseman tumbled to the ice and slid, a whistle shrilled, stopping the play. Turning bewilderedly, Bud saw the referee rotating his clenched fists around one another in front of his chest—the charging signal. The referee pointed to Bud. "Two minutes!" he barked.

"What?" Bud protested.

The referee gave him a stony look. "You took more than two steps, and he didn't even have the puck when you hit him. You want a five-minute misconduct for arguing about it?"

The referee skated toward the judges to inform them and the timekeeper of the penalty. Dupuis came up beside Bud.

"I question the two steps," he began, "but—"

Art Schoen came up. "What's the matter with your eyes, Bud? All he did was deflect that puck! You were asking for a penalty! Nice time to do it!"

Bud moved toward him. "If you're saying—"

Dupuis blocked him. "Heat of the game, *mon ami*. Go to the box."

Sitting down in the penalty box, Bud could feel the sting of Tierney's scowl and looks from the alternate players on the Battler bench.

And then, again, that voice came from high in the stands. "Nice going, Carson!"

Bud bristled but sat perfectly still, jaws clenched.

Lou Huff won the face-off. The Battlers tried to kill the penalty, but the Oilers were in control. The Battlers raced to their defense zone and fought doggedly against the attack. The Calgary team was fired up. Suddenly the puck slammed into the net, and the red light on the scoreboard flashed.

Tie score, 1–1.

The Calgary crowd lifted the roof with their cheers and applause. With the Battlers back to full strength, the Oilers were powering in to get another score, when the buzzer sounded, ending the period.

In the dressing room, nothing was said about Bud's penalty, but he could feel the questioning. Just before the start of the third period, Tierney spoke to the club.

"We're all mad about what's happened," he said. Bud stared at him, but the coach didn't look in his direction. "That's good. It'll help us get back on the aggressive. But let's stay at full strength, and we can lick them. Just take your anger out on the puck and the goal." The players nodded and filed out of the room.

Lou Huff's line took the ice for the third period. The Battlers played carefully, avoiding penalties, but kept losing the puck. Only Chuck Ainsworth's goaltending saved them from a rout. After each save he shouted encouragement at them.

"Stop being namby-pamby, you lugs! Get the lead out! Behind you, Peewee! Watch it! Get it outa here—it ain't quarantined down there!" He caught a flip shot and dropped it for Bud. "Take it away, Bud! I don't want to see it again."

Eluding the defenseman, Bud took the puck over the blue line into the neutral zone. He stickhandled by feel, his eyes not on the puck but on the players.

Lou Huff was outskating the opposing center down the rink. Bud shot the puck to him, and the whistle blasted. The linesman pointed to Lou. An offside—his skates had been just over the blue line before the puck crossed it.

Such things happened. Yet Bud wondered. Last week, in Boise, Lou had been too slow at a crucial moment . . . now, too fast.

Bud coasted by him and spoke without moving his lips. "Let's try the same play we used at the opening."

Lou's expression didn't change.

The referee dropped the puck. Lou got the draw. He shot the puck, but not toward the Battler goal as Bud expected. Lou passed to Rod Stevens, who rammed his way from neutral ice into the attack zone. A moment later, Rod's pass back to Lou was intercepted. Dupuis, skating backward, hip checked his man to the ice and snapped the puck to Bud. A pass to Lou, who took it over the blue line. Art Schoen swooped in and went for the goal; the puck hit the metal post supporting the net and rebounded. Bud raced into the angle of the rebound with a wrist shot, before the goalie could drop in a split. The red light gleamed at 15:07 of the third period. Battlers, 2–1.

The score stayed that way until the final buzzer.

In the dressing room, Lou Huff spoke to Bud. "I was afraid of trying that play toward our own goal. The Oilers were too hot."

"Sure." Bud nodded. "Guess you were right." But still he wondered. He felt certain that the

Oilers would have been caught off guard, expecting the drive toward their goal. The Battlers could have organized a strong play down the ice. Instead, they almost lost possession and possibly the game on the play Lou set up. Dupuis had saved it.

The Battlers spent the night in Calgary. In the morning, their chartered plane flew them to Milwaukee, Wisconsin. From there, a bus took them to nearby Racine for a game that night with the Commandos.

At the hotel in Racine, Gleason grabbed a moment with Bud. "I don't want to seem too chummy with you. People need to think I'm suspecting you, the same as they are—"

"I understand," said Bud.

"Just so you know," Gleason said. "I'm still in the dark about last night. If there was anything we should have spotted in Calgary, I didn't spot it. I tried to tab that heckler, but he kept moving around. I got a pretty fair description of him: redheaded, about five ten, in his thirties. Sound like anyone you might recognize?"

Bud thought for a moment, then shook his head. "I get the impression you think he's more than just a loudmouth."

Gleason nodded. "I found out something else, Bud. Found out too late, because I was asleep at the switch. I should have wondered why a Calgary fan was going out of his way to suggest you were going to throw the game to his club."

"That *is* a point," Bud agreed. "What did you find out?"

"Well, he convinced some of the crowd. Between periods, especially after the Oilers overcame our lead to tie the score, some more money was put on the Calgary club—and lost."

Bud squinted. "Who did the betting on the Battlers? Somebody collected a wad."

"If we knew who, we might know who was fixing some of the games. It's either the redhead or someone he's working for. But I don't think last night's game was fixed. They just figured we had the better chance of winning."

"If that's the case," Bud said, "it kicks the feet out from under some suspicions I got on the ice." He frowned. "I wonder how the betting is on tonight's game."

"From what I've heard, it's pretty even, so far," Gleason replied. He looked at his watch. "I'm going to see the head of security for the rink. I'll want some of his men to help me watch for redheads at the gates tonight."

Bud chuckled, in spite of his feelings. "That's *really* reaching. You can't just walk up to every redhead who comes in and ask—"

"I'm aware of that," Gleason interrupted irritably. "I don't even know how many redheaded hockey fans there are in Racine."

"It's a metropolitan area, close to both Chicago and Milwaukee, and—"

"All right," Gleason snapped. "So I'm reaching. But I might just be lucky enough to grab something. Like maybe a guy who's heckling hard and making a lot of bets. I've got to try, or soon the Battler franchise will be going down the drain—and your reputation and your father's with it."

"I'll keep my eyes open on the ice," Bud promised.

After practice, the Battler club went back to their hotel, had their big meal about two o'clock, and then were ordered to their rooms to rest until close to game time.

Bud shared a room with Dupuis, Lou Huff, and Remy, the second line center. Lou sat at the table, writing a letter. Remy slouched in a chair to watch a TV game show. Bud stretched out on a bed and tried to push the disturbing thoughts out of his mind. He didn't succeed until he began watching Peewee. The big French Canadian sat with pillows propped on the headboard of another bed. He softly hummed a French melody as his huge hands deftly sewed a button on a shirt.

"Such domesticity," Bud laughed. "You remind me of Whistler's Mother. Only you're off your rocker!"

Dupuis shrugged slightly. *"Mon ami,* if you had many brothers and sisters behind you, you also would have become a little mother."

"Little!" Bud guffawed.

Dupuis glanced at him. "It is good to hear you laugh. Now, sleep."

Bud, turning to a more comfortable position, wondered at the brief, curious look from Lou Huff. Was Lou aware of Bud's suspicions—and perhaps pleased that they weren't too deep for laughter?

Bud woke up once, briefly, and saw that the others were dozing or fast asleep. He drifted off again.

Later, he came up slowly from a deep, black well when he heard Dupuis mutter, *"Sacre-bleu!"*

Maybe Peewee was sewing again and had stabbed himself with a needle. . . . Then Bud became aware of a strange voice in the room. Dupuis spoke over it: "Quick—shut that thing off before he hears."

Bud opened his eyes. The room was dim in the twilight, and Lou Huff was shutting off the TV. Bud glimpsed the figure of a man on the screen before the picture compressed down to a bright dot and then went dark.

"What's up?" he asked.

"Nothing," said Dupuis.

Lou Huff was frowning, trying to look as though he hadn't heard. Remy wandered casually toward the bathroom.

"Turn it on again, Lou," Bud said.

Lou was hesitant, glancing at Dupuis. Bud swung off the bed and turned on the set. The figure of the man reappeared on the screen, and his voice came into the room. ". . . so we can expect a very hard-fought game tonight between the Commandos and the Boise Battlers. I'll be back to tell you all about it on the late sports wrap-up."

Bud snapped off the set and faced around. "All right, what did he say?" Dupuis tried to dismiss it with a wave, but Bud wouldn't have it. "You said you didn't want me to hear, so it must have been something about me. What was it?"

Lou looked uncomfortable.

"Speak up," Bud demanded.

Lou spoke, first to Peewee. "He's going to keep at us, and if we don't tell him, he'll imagine it's worse than it is." The center glanced at Bud. "Just the same talk that started in Boise. Very carefully stated, of course, full of 'alleged' and—"

"Never mind," Bud sighed. "I can guess it. Throwing games, huh?"

"Just that *some* people were suspicious," Lou said, looking at the floor. "Nothing has been proved. So far, no action is going to be taken by the governors of the league. The sportscaster did say that you played very well in Calgary, which would tend to offset any rumors. And it's to be expected you'll try to look real good tonight. . . ." Lou hesitated. "The Commandos are proud of their record this season. They'll really be pouring it on, to show that they'll win by ability and not by a . . . a fluke."

Bud's mind raced. Was this sportscast going to build up the betting on the game? Would it keep attention on him and off someone else? He stared at Lou. "And what do you think?"

It was Dupuis who answered, and his expression was not a gentle one. "There is only one answer. We must win."

4
Smothered Suspicion

AT THE FACE-OFF, the Commando center, Wright, got the draw and shot the puck to his left winger, Larson. Just across the blue line, Dupuis closed in like a grizzly and poke checked. He got the puck back into the neutral zone. Before he could pass it to the Battler forward line, he took a shoulder check from Larson that sent him sliding on his back across the ice.

The Racine crowd cheered as the big French Canadian slid. But Larson, undefended, still couldn't deke Chuck. Crouching, the goalie moved out from the goal crease to cut down the angle of the shot. Larson blasted the puck; the *thunk* against Chuck's padded ankle could be heard throughout the arena. Lou Huff swooped in and got the rebound. He passed to Bud. In the neutral zone, Bud swerved toward center ice and wrist shot to Art Schoen. The left winger angled the puck across the blue line for Lou. But Wright, the Commando center, stickhandled it away from him and sent it back toward Larson. Dupuis intercepted.

Bud, Lou, and Art raced to get out of the attack zone, to prevent an offside, before the puck came back. They needn't have worried, though; Larson's stick clashed with Dupuis's. They were jostling over it, when a Commando defense poke checked it out. Wright caught it and whipped it to the right winger. Rod Stevens hip checked him and sent the puck back to Lou.

The Battlers got it to the blue line again; then it went back to their own defense zone. Dupuis and Larson crashed into the sideboards. The only thing Dupuis could do was freeze the puck with his skate.

The face-off was in the red circle to the left of the Battler goal. Lou Huff lost it, and there was a wild melee in front of the goal crease until Chuck froze the puck with his glove.

Another face-off in the Battler defense zone. Lou Huff got the puck to Rod Stevens, who took it into the neutral area. Rod gave it to Art, but the wingman couldn't advance the rubber toward the blue line. He backhanded to Rod, who shunted to Lou. Then the puck came toward Bud. The Commando defenseman, with an astounding spurt, got his stick out and deflected the pass to Larson.

Dupuis gouged ice. He had had the similar intention of intercepting and deflecting the pass away from Larson. Instead, his outthrust stick tangled with Larson's skate. The Commando wing went down headlong to the ice, and the referee's whistle blasted. The referee chopped at his right knee with his hand: tripping. A two-minute penalty.

Bud swung up to the referee. As Battler captain, he had the right to request an explanation of a call on any of his teammates. He maintained that Peewee was merely trying to get the puck.

"He wasn't beside Larson," the referee pointed out. "He was *behind* him." Waving Dupuis to the penalty bench, he left to inform the timekeeper of the penalty. Bud groaned inwardly. It was bad, leaving the Battlers one man short against the powerful Racine team.

Lou Huff won the draw. The Battlers tried, but didn't have a chance to keep the puck. Their only hope was to kill the penalty by fighting off the Commando attack. Sticks clashed. Skates rang. Bodies jostled. The crowd was on its feet roaring at the fracas.

Suddenly the Commandos had the puck inside the Battlers' box defense formation. Wright, from the point, whistled a slap shot. Chuck went down in a split, trying to smother the puck and give his teammates a quick breather. The puck rebounded from his descending glove.

Larson met the rebound and launched a flip shot. Bud had seen his intention. He had no chance to block it with his stick, but if he could get his body in the way—

Someone jostled him, and as he fell, the puck struck him. He landed on it inside the crease. Bud heard the shrilling whistle and some boos from the stands.

No one except the goalie was permitted to smother the puck inside the crease. There were more boos as Bud futilely tried to explain to the referee that he had been pushed. There would be a penalty shot—a rare occurrence—for the Commando wing, whose clear attempt at the goal had been fouled.

As Bud skated slowly to the boards beyond the red line in the neutral zone, he was aware of frowns from Tierney and the Battler bench. Facing the rink, he lined up with Lou Huff, Art Schoen, and Rod Stevens. Dupuis was still in the penalty box. Across the ice, the Racine club lined up.

The referee skated out into the neutral zone and placed the puck at the center face-off circle. Larson, as though he had all the time in the world, leisurely moved out into the neutral ice. The crowd cheered him.

"Sock it to 'em, Swede! Show 'em how it's done!"

Larson went down the rink, almost to his own goal, made a casual skating turn, and came back toward the puck. Chuck Ainsworth crouched, watching from the goal crease. The fans roared as Larson came up on the puck with poised stick. Chuck tensed, but Larson didn't touch the puck —just skated in a circle around it. The crowd laughed. At his own blue line, Larson cut back again, *fast*. Chuck, who had relaxed slightly, tensed again.

Larson swung, but only swished the air above the puck. The crowd guffawed, enjoying the action. Bud knew that Chuck wasn't. Larson's delaying tactics were tightening him, relaxing, tightening; making him overly tense, psyching him off-balance.

At last Larson moved the puck. Amid shouts from the stands, he stickhandled it on a weaving course toward the goal. Chuck waited, crouching, watching the puck. His skates were about shoulder width apart, toes turning out slightly; his stick was poised on the ice in front of the skates. The big glove he held to the left and a bit forward, with the palm facing outward, set to make a catch.

Larson stickhandled over the blue line. The crowd quieted, holding its collective breath. Larson, skating fast, suddenly moved his head to the right for a turn in that direction. Instead he snapped it back for a swerve to his left.

Chuck didn't move, refusing to be deked.

Larson must have realized that; he kept the puck on the right side, ahead of him, then wrist shot powerfully.

Thunk! The fans yelped when the rear of the net bulged outward. But the bulge was caused by Chuck's skates as they shot backward when he fell on his face, his hands well outside the goal. He lifted his glove high, turned it over, and dumped the puck onto the ice outside the goal crease.

The crowd gasped and groaned.

"Magnifique!" Dupuis shouted.

"Beautiful!" Bud exclaimed.

From the stands, the crowd now applauded Chuck's save. Larson shook his head in disbelief and gave Chuck a smile.

Play resumed with a face-off, with Dupuis back in for the Battlers. The back and forth struggle resumed, but the period ended with no score.

In the dressing room, Tierney made only one comment about the first period: "They took the momentum from us, but we stopped it dead. Now, let's get it back and keep it. Get jumping out there."

The Commandos were equally determined to regain the edge of momentum, and the second period buzzer sounded with no score by either club.

At 5:07 of the third session, from twenty feet

out, a whizzing, bouncing flip shot leaped over the goalie's glove and into the Commando net. The Battlers crowded around Lou Huff, thumping his shoulders.

Boise, 1–0.

The Commandos lived up to their name, making repeated commando raids on the Battler goal. Chuck Ainsworth stood off the barrage of pucks. Then, at 19:41, with only nineteen seconds of play remaining, he made another save and got the rubber to Rod Stevens. The left defense passed to Lou in the neutral zone. Lou stick-handled across the blue line. Art Schoen evaded his defenseman at the boards and raced into the attack zone. He caught a pass from Lou and whammed the puck past the goalie and into the narrow opening at the far corner of the goal.

That clinched the game for the Battlers in the dwindling seconds of the final period.

Larson, pulling off his glove and holding out his hand, swept up to Bud as the buzzer sounded. "Pretty hot. It's a wonder the ice didn't melt."

"We all tried," Bud agreed.

In the dressing room a few minutes later, Sid Seidler, the syndicated sportswriter, tossed his expensive Tyrolean hat ceilingward. "Man, did you Battlers live up to your name!" He thrust through the exuberant players to Chuck Ainsworth. "Congratulations! Do you know that you're the first goalie in three years to shut out the Commandos?"

Seidler went round the room, seeking out each player who had participated in the win. Bud scarcely heard the remarks directed to him. He drew Seidler to one side.

"Sid, did you spot who pushed me into the crease?"

Seidler stared at him. "Has someone already suggested that you deliberately—"

"Not yet. But in light of past experience, I'm anticipating it. If I can confirm that I was pushed. . . ."

"It was a boiling pack, Bud." Seidler frowned, trying to recall. "Just about impossible to see who was who and who was doing what. The only chance to find out would be with a slow playback of a TV tape." He shook his head. "I didn't see any cameras spotted around. Of course, there might have been someone on hand with a portable for a couple of spot shots. I'll check and see."

"Thanks," said Bud. "The club will be leaving for Lansing as soon as we pack our gear. If there is a tape available, I could stay over and take a commercial flight later."

Seidler nodded. "I'll let you know. Keep your skates sharp, Bud."

Turning, Bud saw Rod Stevens staring at him. He hesitated, then spoke. "Did you overhear what I said to Sid?"

The defenseman nodded.

"Well, can *you* give me an answer?"

There was a long moment before Stevens shook his head, then pulled his jersey up over his head and turned away.

Dupuis murmured to Bud, "He thinks he knows the answer. He doesn't think you were pushed. At least, he didn't say it out loud."

"Not this time," Bud muttered. "But sooner or later, someone on the club is going to say it, just like the fans." Bud sat down and thumped his fist on the bench. "Nice, isn't it? The two guys I suspected"—he glanced at Art and Lou— "saved the game that it looks as if I tried to throw."

"I did not do much to help us win," Dupuis said, smiling crookedly.

"You? How do you come into this?"

Dupuis lifted his thick, dark eyebrows, then

let them drop. "I am your very close *ami,* like a brother." He spoke wryly. "My accidentally deliberate tripping of Larson and the penalty—"

"That could have happened to anybody," Bud protested.

"*Oui,* but we are no longer anybodies. We are somebodies—to suspect."

"Who said—"

Dupuis put out his hand to keep Bud seated as he started to stand up. "No one has said—yet. I just feel it here." Dupuis patted his chest.

Bud was the last of the team to board the charter plane that would take them to Lansing, Michigan. He looked back at the deserted boarding area. No sign of Seidler bringing word about a TV tape. No airline attendant hurrying with a message for Bud Carson.

"Are you with us, Bud?" Gleason called from the door of the plane while a stewardess and attendant waited to close it. Bud joined the club owner in the vestibule just aft of the cockpit.

"I didn't hear the redhead tonight."

"If he showed, he kept quiet," Gleason agreed. "Wasn't any need for him to sound off, after those innuendos on the air and in the late-after-

noon papers." Gleason smiled grimly. "The fools
who bet on that kind of information lost it this
time."

"Thanks to our center, left wing, and goalie."
Bud then asked Gleason if he had noted anything significant in the action at the Commando
goal crease.

"That's like asking me to find a needle in a
haystack."

Bud nodded disconsolately. On his way to his
seat near the rear of the plane, he noticed that
the other club members carefully avoided looking at him.

In the Michigan game, the Lancer center
spearheaded action in the second period that
netted a goal. But that scarcely dented the Battlers' three goals, which increased to five before
the final buzzer.

Two nights later, in Hamilton, Ontario, the
Battlers clipped the wings of the Hawks 4–2.

Swinging homeward, they shut out the Sioux
Falls Indians 3–0. In Rapid City, the Raiders
should have hidden out in the Badlands. After
ten minutes of the first period, Tierney kept
Remy's line and the second defense line on the

ice for an 8–0 shutout. He said he was saving the first six for the big game with the Vikings on the home rink.

Shortly before their plane landed at Boise, Tierney spoke to the club over the intercom.

"We've got two days until we meet the Vikings. You can have tomorrow off, but don't overdo anything."

Club members laughed, adding comments of their own.

"All right," Tierney continued. "Just remember that we stand fourth in the league toward the end-of-season play-offs. Let's not jeopardize that. Friday, we'll practice hard. I'll let you know then whether we'll have a light practice Saturday morning."

Though the hour was late when the plane landed, there was a crowd of fans waiting at the Boise airport, along with some newsmen. Bud braced himself for hostile questions about his actions in the Racine game, but there were none. A few fans asked him for his autograph. He felt good riding out toward East Boise with his sister and Dupuis. His sister had a late snack waiting.

"That game with the Commandos!" she exclaimed later. "I nearly died, Bud, when you smothered the puck in the crease!"

Bud didn't pick up the coffee cup he was grasping, and Dupuis paused in the midst of compiling his fourth bologna, cheese, and lettuce sandwich.

"Did you see it happen?" Bud asked, his eyes sharp.

"No, the announcer just mentioned it on a late sportscast. They did run a film clip of that cat-and-mouse penalty shot."

Bud frowned. He supposed that on a general sportscast there was a limited amount of footage that could be shown on any single event. Yet, in light of the rumors concerning him, there might be a shot of the foul. . . .

"What channel was that on?" Bud asked.

His sister told him, then glanced at the clock. "But it's after midnight. The late movie's finishing up."

Bud went to the phone and called the station, anyway. The man he spoke to hadn't been working on the night of the Racine game, and there was no one else at the studio who had been there.

"I doubt if we have a full tape," the technician explained. "It was probably shot to us from the network via microwave or coaxial cable. Our sports director would know how much he recorded and used. You can call him tomorrow. He'll be in about one thirty."

"Banker's hours," Bud commented, with a disappointed snort.

"No sports events in the morning," came the reply. "Sorry. That's all the help I can give you."

Getting ready for bed, still finishing yet another sandwich, Dupuis shook his head.

"I hope with you, naturally," he said. "But if there *is* something on tape, what will it show? Maybe a Commando bumping you in. Perhaps deliberately—it has been done. But he would claim accident. And if it shows that Art or Lou did it—" Dupuis lifted his hands and let them drop. "Then why did they later save the game for us?"

"You're a big help," Bud muttered. "But there's still Rod Stevens. I didn't like the way he evaded answering my questions about it after the game."

"Maybe he did not know," Dupuis said. "One thing *I* know: I do not like the way you burden your mind with suspicions. It is not good for you or your playing."

Bud chuckled. "You should be the last one to talk about 'burdening'!" He pointed at the remaining bit of Dupuis's fifth sandwich on the corner of the dresser.

Dupuis pretended to pout as he settled down in his twin bed.

"I'm still your friend," Bud assured him. "I'm also your captain, and I'm warning you now that we're going down to Julia Davis Park tomorrow morning and run off your fat."

In the morning, there were four inches of snow.

"Good," said Peewee, turning back to bed. "No running."

"Skiing," said Bud. "Let's go!"

At Bogus Basin, in the mountains above Boise, Bud parked beside a low-slung crimson sports coupe.

"I wonder what that hunk of machinery costs," he mused.

"Enough," said Dupuis, "to feed my brothers and sisters for two years. Feast only your eyes, *mon ami*. Such cannot be yours until you play in the majors."

"And that may *never* be," said Bud.

They unpacked their gear and bought tickets

for the ski lifts. Soon Dupuis was whooping and singing as he streaked down the slopes. He shouted to other skiers as he swooped past. Glancing back at an attractive young woman, he tried to make an abrupt stop and stumbled in a cloud of powder snow.

Bud, laughing, came to a graceful stop beside him. "What were you trying to do," Bud inquired, "practice back skiing and a hip check?"

Dupuis, looking like a huge snowman, got back up on his skis. He brushed off the snow, then looked over Bud's shoulder with eyebrows raised.

"*Bon jour*," he said rather coldly. Turning, Bud found himself looking at Sid Seidler.

"Well," the sportswriter greeted them, "I know you fellows have to stay in condition, but this—"

Dupuis interrupted, and if words had shoulders there would have been a chip on each one. "Why did you not inform Bud that there was a tape of that Racine game?" He looked like a snowy bear about to charge.

Seidler's eyes were unreadable behind his dark glasses. Bud saw his mittened hand tighten and lift a ski pole slightly, as though he might have to use it to defend himself.

"What's the accusing tone for?" Sid inquired.

"Easy, Peewee," Bud cautioned, watching the sportswriter. "I'd like to know, too. Why didn't you let me know?"

"For one very simple reason," Seidler retorted. "I checked up on a possible tape, as I promised you. The cameraman used a portable, and all he had taken were some spot shots. He didn't get the action around the goal crease during your foul. He was about to leave to get back to the studio for the late news roundup. He stayed to shoot the penalty shot. There wasn't any point in my rushing to the airport to tell you that. I thought you'd assume, since you hadn't heard from me—"

"Sorry," Bud said, glancing at Dupuis, who nodded slightly.

Seidler relaxed, but his tone was curt. "Let me give you a bit of advice. I understand your position and your feelings, Bud. But you aren't going to improve anything by being so fast with the accusations."

"I wasn't accusing, Sid. I was just asking why—"

"Is there a difference?" Seidler demanded, looking from Bud to Dupuis. He dug in his ski poles and went on down the slope.

Bud and Dupuis went down more leisurely and in silence. They were removing their skis, when another familiar face—Rod Stevens—appeared out of the crowd.

"I didn't know you guys were up here," Rod said. "We could have been skiing together. How long have you been here?"

"Long enough," said Bud. "See you."

As Bud and Dupuis approached the parking area, they heard the snarl of a powerful car. It was the crimson sports job, and at the wheel was Sid Seidler. With tires flinging back snow, the car fishtailed and then surged away down the road.

"Even his car sounds mad," said Dupuis. "I guess he still is, too."

Bud nodded. "Let's hope he gets over it when he cools down. It doesn't pay to have a well-known sportswriter down on you, and we need all the support we can get."

5
Thin Ice

THERE HAD BEEN an intensive practice on Friday, but Tierney called for a brief session on Saturday, ahead of the bantams. Coaches frequently did this on the day of an important game; a light session of checking and stickhandling helped to relax tensions and loosen up the players.

Bud and Dupuis rose early Saturday morning. Bud brought in the morning paper while Peewee was being domestic again, singing softly as he cooked breakfast.

After Bud skimmed the usual headlines about

prices, taxes, political scandals, and international tensions, he turned to the sports section. He saw Sid Seidler's column, SEIDLER'S SIDELIGHTS. The article was subheaded *Let's Keep It on Ice,* and it read:

In contrast to other pro sports, such as baseball, football, and basketball, the sometimes bloodied rinks of ice hockey have remained amazingly free of inroads by organized gambling. Not that hockey is a parlor game. Next to boxing, ice hockey is one of the most punishing of physical contact sports. In pro hockey, players collide —intentionally—at speeds up to forty miles per hour, and hard rubber pucks become missiles that have been clocked at one hundred miles per.

Surgeons and dentists get plenty of work rebuilding the heads and front teeth of hockey players, yet the repairers of halos, if there be such, find little or no work in that sport. The scarred and porcelain-toothed players of pro hockey have, for the most part, kept their halos undented and untarnished by the scandal of gambling influence.

There have been a few blemishes, as there always are where competition and money get together. Two players of the NHL were once outlawed from the game by the governor of the league for consorting with known gamblers. The late Bart Carson, an organizer, coach, and player of the Boise Battlers, died last season under a cloud of suspicion—suspicion which has been neither dispelled nor confirmed. However, the record books and the known character of the man should suffice to dissipate any stigma from his name.

Wisps of that cloud linger, and they have wafted in the direction of Bart Carson's son, Bud, captain and right wing of the Battler club. In a way, the situation is inescapable for Bud Carson. Hockey fans are the most vociferous of sports spectators, and they shout first and think later.

Of course, Bud has objected. Who wouldn't? But the assault-and-battery nature of the game can make a player look bad when he isn't. He can also look good. And, except for one brief incident on the Battlers' recent out-of-town schedule, Bud Carson has looked very good. That's what he should continue to do: play the game, to the best of his ability. Let actions speak louder than words. Otherwise, to paraphrase Shakespeare, we may think the man protests too much—as though he really has something to hide.

Hockey's a great sport. Aside from occasional spilled blood, which is part of the game, let's keep it that way.

Let's keep bad blood out of it. Let's keep it on ice.

Bud breathed hard but put a check on what he wanted to say. He tossed the paper to Dupuis as he sat down at the table.

"What do you make of that?"

Dupuis read, now and then nodding in agreement or murmuring, *"Oui,"* but halfway through the column, he began to scowl.

"Sacre-bleu!" he muttered, reading the final words. When he looked up, his eyes were glowing

hotly. "It is dirty writing. He pretends to whiten you, but he leaves some smudges."

Bud nodded. "I was afraid of something like this, after what happened at Bogus Basin. I guess it's true that 'the pen is mightier than the sword.'"

"*Non!*" Dupuis growled. "He will know different when I let him feel a hockey stick."

Bud shook his head slowly. "The best thing we can do is to ignore it. Let it wither and die. He's definitely right about one thing: The more we protest, the worse we'll look."

"But if we do nothing," Dupuis objected, "it will look like we have no defense."

"The only defense we do have is how we play," Bud pointed out.

"And," Dupuis growled, "now everyone will be watching closely to see something wrong."

"That can't be helped." Bud frowned. "But at the same time, we'll still be watching to see who *does* do something wrong."

At the brief Saturday morning practice, Bud sensed a new restraint among some members of the club. Others tried to make light of Seidler's column.

"Stay out of the goal crease tonight, Bud!"

He stifled his resentment and smiled.

Someone else called out, "Don't *anyone* get any penalties tonight. It may dent your halo!"

Tierney scowled. "Lay off that kind of talk. We're ready for the Vikings, and we're going to play tough. Everyone out on the ice!" Tierney ordered. He paused by Bud. "What the devil brought this on from Seidler?"

"A lot of things, I guess."

"I can imagine," the coach retorted. "Try to keep your mind on the game tonight."

When practice was over the bantams arrived. Mark Strickland came skating down the rink toward Bud.

"Mr. Carson, watch!" He made a sweeping turn and skated all the way around it, instead of gliding.

"Good!" Bud called. "Now let's see it to the right. . . . Not bad. Keep working at that right turn."

Mark's parents had come around the side of the rink. Mrs. Strickland's brassy hair looked as though it had been varnished into place. "Thank you for suggesting figure skating," she said. "It's really helped Mark."

Her husband nodded. "Kind of stretched the

budget, but it's been worth it."

"Mark," Mrs. Strickland called, moving away, "the tape's coming loose on your stick. Come over here and I'll fix it for you."

Wayne Strickland stepped closer to Bud and lowered his voice. "Don't let on to my wife, but I've stretched things a little further to put a good bet on you fellows for tonight."

"Hope it's one you can afford to lose," Bud said. Strickland's gaze deepened. "We'll do our best," Bud continued. "We always do. But hockey is an uncertain game."

"I know," Strickland murmured. "Seidler's column this morning mentioned some of the uncertainties—"

"I saw it," Bud broke in. He stepped away to join Mrs. Strickland and Mark. "Once the tape comes loose, it's better to replace it," he said. "And don't use white tape, Mark. It makes it too easy for the goalie to keep his eye on the puck."

"Dad," Mark called, "have you got any black tape in the car?"

His father shook his head.

Bud reached for the stick. "While Dupuis is giving you fellows a skating drill, I'll rewind it for you." He raised his voice to the other bantams. "Anyone else got a stick that needs taping?"

Several were eagerly offered to him.

Dupuis laughed. *"Mon ami,* maybe someday you will learn to keep your mouth closed." Peewee blew a whistle, then waved to the bantams. *"Allons-y!"* They raced after him as he started around the rink.

"He looks like a papa panda with cubs," Bud remarked. He went to the dressing room with the bantams' sticks.

A few club members, changing to street clothes after practice, eyed the smaller sticks and kidded Bud about being sent down to the minor-*minor* league. Bud hoped it was as good-natured in intention as it sounded.

At the sturdy worktable, which held tools and the grinder for sharpening skates, he stripped off the old tapes from the small sticks. He cut new lengths of black tape, then wound them carefully and snugly on the sticks' blades.

As he was leaving the dressing room, he saw Tierney coming through the players' doorway to Gleason's office.

"Bud," the coach called, "Tex wants to see you when it's convenient. I was just going out to the ice to tell you."

"Right now, or after the bantams finish practice?" Bud asked.

"Wait." Tierney opened the office door. "Tex, Bud's down here now. He's got the kids on the ice and wants to know how long—" Tierney stopped and motioned Bud toward the office. He held the door open for Bud and moved as though he were going to enter the office, too.

"Thanks, Al." Gleason was dismissing him. "I think you've got a good plan in the lineup for tonight."

Bud joined Gleason at the big window. The club owner-manager sighed heavily and rocked on the heels of his cowboy boots. He nodded toward the telephone.

"I had a call from the league governor this morning. He'd read Seidler's column in a Toronto paper and wanted to know the basis for it."

Bud stood rigidly silent. Was he going to be told that he was being suspended, pending an investigation?

"I had to be frank with him, Bud," Gleason continued. "It would have looked bad for the entire club if I'd kept mum. I was hoping this could be cleared up within the club, but it's gotten outside now."

"You had no choice but to be honest with the governor," Bud agreed.

"I sweated it for a moment," Gleason admitted. "I reminded him about the circumstances of Bart's death after a spotless record. I told him it was only some sorehead fans shifting that blot to you." Gleason hesitated. "I admitted that there were some circumstances, in some games, that *might* be questioned. And even though we had no real basis for thinking anything was wrong, we were keeping our eyes open."

"We?" Bud questioned.

Gleason nodded. "I told him of your feelings about Bart's death."

"I figured that," Bud said. "By 'we' I meant did you mention anyone else?"

"No. You and I were the only ones in the club that I named. Why did you ask, Bud?"

"I was just wondering if, in your mind, you might have cleared anyone I'd be apt to suspect."

Gleason looked straight at him. "In my mind, everyone in this club is clear until I've got reason to believe otherwise. There may be something going on; I feel there very likely is. But if I start looking too hard for it, without good cause, I'll only be ripping the club apart at the seams. Do you understand my position?"

Bud nodded, feeling uneasy about some of his suspicions.

"As far as I'm concerned, it's still the same set-up," Gleason went on. "You get any suspicions, you tell them to *me*. No one else, except maybe Dupuis. But warn him to go easy, too." Gleason sighed. "Now you better get back to your bantams, before they tear up the rink."

"Just one more thing," Bud said. "What did you tell the governor about me? I mean, about the implications in Seidler's column."

"I said that Seidler had it right. Except for that incident in the crease, which could have happened to anyone, you played very well on the tour."

"Thanks," said Bud, turning toward the door.

Gleason called after him. "Watch yourself, Bud. Try to avoid any more bad-looking predicaments like that one in the crease."

Bud smiled wryly. "That proves you're not a hockey player, boss, or you'd know that's easier said than done."

As Bud stepped into the corridor, he saw Tierney coming out of his office.

"Tex still here?"

Bud nodded, wondering at the coach's worried frown. He held the door open for Tierney, who began speaking before he was fully into Gleason's office.

"Chuck's father is in the hospital again. Intensive care. Chuck's standing by there. He phoned to let me know that if things don't improve—"

"He won't show for the game tonight," Gleason surmised. "Well, that's understandable. But Palmer should be able to handle the goal."

Palmer was the Battlers' second goalie and was as capable as Chuck.

Gleason frowned. "Who else are you going to suit up?"

League rules required that there must always be a substitute goalie on the team bench, suited up in his cumbersome gear and ready to take to the ice. The Battlers had two more men in training, but they weren't ready to face a contingent like the Vancouver Vikings.

"If necessary," Tierney said, "I'll suit up myself. I'm listed as a player-coach."

"All right," Gleason agreed, "but I hope it doesn't come to that. I'd prefer you on the bench, where you can keep a better eye on what has to be done to lock up the Vikings."

"Speaking of locks," Tierney said, turning to Bud, "you didn't lock the dressing room when you left a minute ago." His tone was critical.

"Oh," Bud replied, "I'll—"

"Never mind," the coach cut in. "I saw to it."

"Thanks." As he closed the office door, Bud heard Gleason asking if Chuck needed financial help.

When the bantam session was over, Bud and Dupuis returned to the dressing room to change. The door was unlocked. Bud frowned—hadn't Tierney said he'd locked it? Pushing it open, he saw two men of the maintenance staff cleaning the room.

Bud nudged Peewee and nodded toward one of the men swishing a mop. "Look at that backhand!"

Dupuis tossed an empty soapbox to the floor, and an impromptu hockey game ensued, with mops and sticks. The door from the corridor opened, and Doc Taylor, the club doctor, stood there, shaking his graying head.

"Don't you guys get enough on the ice? It must be a virus." He smiled at the maintenance men. "I suppose soon you'll be trading in your

mops for hockey sticks and skates."

"No, sir!" said one. "I've had to clean up too much blood from the floor in here."

His partner nodded toward Bud and Dupuis. "Let them spill it while I fill my wallet." He hesitated. "I wasn't going to bet on you guys after the last home game. Guess that loss was just a fluke, though, huh?"

"One of those things," Bud answered.

"Who are you betting on tonight?" Doc Taylor inquired, moving toward the adjoining dispensary with boxes of supplies.

"The Battlers! I'd be a fool not to, after the showing they made on the road."

"Thanks," Bud murmured. "We'll try not to let you down."

Doc was still stocking his cabinet and kit for the night's game when Bud and Dupuis were ready to leave.

"Will you lock up, Doc?" Bud asked.

"You take care of the dressing room," the doctor answered, setting the lock on the connecting door. "I'll go out from here."

On the way home for the big meal of the day and some rest before the game, Bud drove absentmindedly and nearly ran a red light.

Dupuis raised his dark eyebrows. "If you play without paying attention tonight, that porter is going to go after you with his mop."

"That's what I was thinking about," Bud responded. "He said he'd be a fool not to bet on us, after the showing we'd made on the road. The *good* showing—one that rebuilds confidence in the club after a loss. Think back, Peewee. This season and last season. I realize we can't win every game, of course, but haven't our most unexpected losses always happened after a good streak of wins? Don't you see a pattern?"

Dupuis stared ahead through the windshield, then nodded slowly. "*Oui.*" He nodded vigorously. "*Oui, oui!*" He turned toward Bud. His eyes gleamed through narrowed lids. "And tonight, you are thinking, it could be set for us to lose."

"The time's ripe for it," Bud answered through tense lips.

He turned the wheel suddenly to change lanes. There was a squeal of tires and a horn blast from behind as Bud swung into a service station and stopped by the phone booth. He got out of the car and called Gleason.

"You going to be there in the office for a little

while longer?" Bud asked anxiously.

"I was just leaving. You sound excited. What's up?"

"I don't want to talk on the phone," Bud said. "Where can I meet you?"

"Not here," Gleason said. "The Vikings have arrived."

Bud understood. The Vikings would be having a brief practice, to loosen up from their trip and to get the feel of the rink, especially puck ricochets from the boards. The Vikings wouldn't run through any secret new plays, but as a gesture of courtesy, no members of the Battler club would be present in the building.

"I'm heading for home," Gleason told Bud. "Suppose you meet me halfway." He named a restaurant near the foot of Bogus Basin Road.

Fifteen minutes later, in the restaurant booth, Bud outlined his thoughts about a series of wins, then an arranged loss—a possible pattern of fixed games.

Gleason was silent for a moment. "It sounds plausible," he said slowly. "If we lost consistently, nobody would ever bet on us." He pursed his lips. "Offhand, I'd say there *has* seemed to be a pattern for the last season and for this one, so far." Although his cup of coffee was untouched, Gleason beckoned the waitress to bring the check. "I'm going back downtown. Maybe I can find out what group is doing the heaviest betting on the Vikings for tonight."

Rising, he led the way outside. In the icy parking lot, he tugged the Stetson down a little, against the cold wind blowing off the snowcapped mountains.

"As I said before, Bud, there's got to be someone from the club, too. Maybe, just in case, I ought to advise Tierney to keep you out of the game tonight."

Bud felt apprehension stab through him. "But we'll need all the strength we can get against the Vikings—"

"*Oui!*" Dupuis agreed.

"It's just that if we *do* lose," Gleason went on, "no one could say that you threw the game."

Bud thought that over for a moment, then shook his head. "On the other hand, that could give strength to the rumors about me. It might suggest that I was kept off the ice because I *am* under suspicion."

"You've got a point there." Gleason frowned. "Let's leave everything as is, at least until game time. We can make the decision then."

On the way home again, Bud muttered to Dupuis, "No matter what we do, I'm skating on thin ice."

6
Broken Defense

IT SEEMED TO BUD that there were more Boise
police and Ada County sheriff's deputies than
usual on duty at the rink that evening. He wondered if that had any connection with Gleason's
queries about organized gambling.

At the moment, however, Bud's biggest concern was whether or not he was going to be al-
lowed to play. In the dressing room, he tensely
consulted the bulletin board. His name was on
the list of the seventeen players permitted on the
bench during a game. At least he'd made it that

far. He began suiting up, drawing in his stomach muscles in an effort to stop the butterflies.

Beside him, Dupuis hummed softly, but there didn't seem to be much tune or lilt to it. Some of the players were silent; others chattered. Remy, center of the second forward line, with only one skate on, was sitting very still looking somewhat green. Bud began to feel queasy himself as he thought of what might go wrong tonight. If he made any mistake that looked bad, and the team lost the game. . . .

He had to get his mind off such things. He looked around and saw Chuck suiting up in his heavy gear. Evidently he didn't have to stay at the hospital with his father. But his drawn face and worried eyes suggested that he might end up needing a hospital bed himself.

Tierney came to the door and counted the heads of those suiting up. The referee appeared behind him and handed him a paper—probably the starting lineup of the visiting team. The coach, studying it, moved away toward Gleason's office. Bud breathed deeply and tried to project his thoughts into the manager-owner's office. *Put me in the starting lineup, please. If you don't, it'll start more talk about me.*

The two clubs went out for the pregame warm-up, each taking an end of the rink and avoiding an area thirty feet wide across the center of the neutral zone . . . skating, stickhandling, shooting for the goal to give the goalies some warm-up.

Bud heard Mark Strickland's voice from the stands.

"Hi, Mr. Carson!" Mark sat in the third row, with his parents. Bud lifted his stick slightly; Mrs. Strickland smiled, and her husband waved.

When the fifteen-minute warm-up period was over, the teams returned to their dressing rooms. Rink attendants prepared to resurface the ice.

Tierney announced the starting lineup. "The Vikings are starting with their first forward and defense lines. We'll do the same."

Bud let out his breath. He was in. The coach continued, looking at Bud.

"If we draw any penalties"—his gaze shifted to Art Schoen and Lou Huff—"come off the ice."

They nodded, knowing that the special squad of penalty killers would go in to block a Viking power play.

"Watch it for the first few minutes," Tierney warned. "Don't try anything dramatic until your tension has settled down. Then—"

A buzzer sounded in the dressing room; the game timekeeper was summoning the clubs to the ice.

"Then," Tierney went on, "let's grab the momentum and hang on to it. All right, let's get at it!"

As Bud skated into position for the opening face-off, Mark Strickland called to him again. Bud nodded, but he didn't move his stick. He was taking no chances that the referee or a linesman might misinterpret any move he made. Mark turned excitedly to the man seated beside him, then pointed toward Bud.

Lou Huff won the draw, sending the puck to Art Schoen, who lost it almost immediately on a poke check. The Viking defense passed to his center, who took it out of the neutral zone and into the Battler defense area. Dupuis deflected a shot at the goal to Lou. The center stickhandled into the neutral zone and passed to Art. The Battler left wing shot it back as soon as he received it, then was tumbled to the ice by a hip check.

The crowd cheered. That had been fast thinking on Art's part, realizing he wouldn't be able to avoid the check. Meanwhile, Lou made a tight, fast circle to elude the Viking center, then angled the puck across the blue line into the attack zone. He shot for the goal. The puck whacked loudly against the goalie's stick, and Bud raced in to meet the rebound. He wrist shot and flipped the puck over the goalie's stick and leg. The goal judge switched on the red light. The Boise fans went wild.

Bud was elated. It was nice to hear cheers instead of boos! He skated to neutral ice for a face-off and spotted Mark on his feet, yelling and waving both hands above his head. Wayne Strickland wore a broad grin. The man on the other side of Mark stared at Bud and nodded as Mark excitedly spoke to him again.

In spite of eighteen more minutes of hard, exciting action, the period ended with the score remaining in the Battlers' favor, 1–0.

In the dressing room, Bud saw Chuck Ainsworth and Rod Stevens in what appeared to be a heated discussion. "What's the problem?" he asked.

Rod shook his head. "I was just telling Chuck that no news is good news from the hospital. He thinks that if word does come, he won't be told until after the game."

Bud frowned. No player could leave the bench during a game unless he required special attention from the doctor in the dressing room.

"I'll speak to Tierney and Gleason," Bud promised. "If word comes, and if you're needed at the hospital, we'll make arrangements to let you go between the second and third periods."

"Thanks, Bud," Rod said. He sat down beside Chuck. "Look, your father's had other attacks worse than this one. He'll be okay. I know he'll pull through."

When the second period began, the rink had been shaved and re-iced by the Zamboni machine. Again, it was a racing battle up and down the rink. At 07:03, the Vikings netted the puck. Tie score, 1–1.

A few minutes later, Art Schoen, racing with the puck, got a rolling hip check. He sprawled on the ice, sliding, and slammed headlong against the boards. He staggered to his skates with blood streaming down the side of his face from a cut forehead.

Bud yelled to him, "Art, get out!" He glanced toward the bench and saw that Tierney had Remy waiting by the gate to come in for Art.

The left defense of the Vikings dug the puck

out of the corner, unhampered by Schoen, who was skating groggily toward the bench.

Bud shouted again. "Defense, watch it!"

Lou Huff streaked down center ice to join forces with Dupuis and Stevens for the defense of the goal. As soon as the Battlers regained the puck, Bud heard a linesman's whistle, stopping the play. Remy had been overzealous about getting out on the ice. He had opened the gate for Art and stepped out onto the ice a shade too soon.

The linesman spoke to the referee, who turned as Bud skated up to him. "Too many men on the ice, captain. Minor bench penalty. Who'll take it for your club?"

Bud glanced toward the bench.

Tierney called out to him, "Give Lou a breather."

Remy was in to take Art's place while the doctor patched him up. Lou Huff took the club's bench penalty, which wouldn't be entered on his individual record.

Bud took the face-off when play resumed. The Battlers, one man short, couldn't retain possession of the puck. They quickly formed a box defense to stave off a Viking power play.

In the midst of the fracas, Bud got the puck.

He ragged it, skating in fast, tight circles, zig-zagging. He couldn't get clear of the Vikings surrounding him or get the rubber to one of his teammates for a breakaway. The Boise fans were on their feet, screaming encouragement to Bud as he killed the penalty. He wondered how many more seconds remained of the two minutes before the Battlers would be back to full strength.

Suddenly a Viking went down to one knee, making a sweep check that knocked Bud's stick up and skittered the puck away. Another Viking shot for the goal. Chuck deflected with his pad, and a Viking stick met the rebound. Chuck went down in a split for another save. Then a flip shot got by him. The red light came on just as Lou raced from the penalty box, too late to help.

Vikings 2, Battlers 1.

In the third row of the stands, the man sitting beside Mark Strickland watched impassively. Mark gave Bud a worried smile; Wayne Strickland just looked worried.

As Bud glanced about, making certain the Battlers were in position for the face-off, he saw Chuck looking at the scoreboard. A few minutes later, there was another face-off because of an

offside, and Bud saw Chuck looking at the board again. Chuck was watching the clock, worried about word from the hospital.

At 18:03 of the second period, the Vikings scored again. On the way to the dressing room at the end of the period, Bud touched Tierney's arm.

"I don't think Chuck's mind is on the game," Bud said. "I can't blame him, under the circumstances, but—"

Tierney nodded. "He's been watching the clock instead of the puck. I've already decided to keep him on the bench."

Gleason came from his office. "Bud," he called.

Bud walked on his skates to the owner's office.

"I'll skip the details about what I did downtown this afternoon," Gleason began.

"I noticed extra police," Bud said. "Have they spotted any gambling?"

"I don't know yet. But they can't pick anyone up for just making a remark like 'I'll bet you a hundred bucks.' The police actually have to witness money being exchanged."

Bud grimaced. "That makes it kind of tough."

"All we can hope for," Gleason said, "is that we might get a line on who's doing the most betting. From what we've learned, there's a lot riding on this game."

"And the game is going just the way someone wants it to," Bud said with a scowl.

"We've got to recover and hit them where it hurts in this next period," Gleason stated flatly. Bud nodded.

In the dressing room, Bud waited, listening as the coach outlined a defense against a particular Viking play. Then Tierney eyed Bud.

"You got anything special to say?"

Bud wondered if the coach expected some hint about the brief confab with Gleason.

"We need three goals—" he began.

Someone jeered. "Tell us something we don't know!"

"I'll tell you something the Vikings don't know," Bud retorted. "We've only been *practicing* in the first and second periods. Now we're ready to go out there and live up to our name. Let's go, Battlers!"

"*Allons-y!*" Dupuis shouted, rising to his skates and holding his stick aloft like a sabre.

Others joined him in the gesture as the timekeeper's warning summoned them back to the ice and the contest.

The Vikings also came out fired up. In the first two minutes, the puck rarely got beyond either blue line.

Dupuis staved off a Viking attack with a shoulder check that knocked the breath out of his man. He passed the puck to Bud; Bud deflected to Lou, who ragged in center ice then shot it over the blue line. Bud swooped toward the puck. The Viking goalie moved out to cut down the angle of opening for Bud, and Bud, swerving toward him, skimmed his stick over the puck but didn't touch it. The puck was there for a drop pass for Lou; Bud screened the goalie's view of him. Lou fired it cleanly into a corner of the net.

The red light glowed; the stands went wild. Vikings 3, Battlers 2.

"One down," Bud called to his teammates, "two to go!"

The Battlers swirled into position for the face-off. Bud glanced quickly about. The Battlers were ready to be in motion for the play Lou launched from the face-off. Even Palmer, the goalie who had replaced Chuck, was crouched and ready. The Vikings seemed equally alert.

Bud waggled his stick blade back and forth on the ice, as if to loosen up his wrists. He hoped that Lou spotted this signal for a special play. Lou gave no indication.

The referee dropped the puck between the two centers. As it hit the ice, Bud drove into action. Lou got the draw, took the puck back, then angled it ahead of Bud. Art eluded his defense and sped diagonally toward center ice. The play called for him to receive the rubber from Bud and take it over the blue line. The goalie would expect a shot from Art at the goal, but Art would drop it and screen the goalie while either Lou or Bud picked it up to shoot for the goal.

Bud spotted a slight shift of the goalie's head as Art moved diagonally in the neutral ice. Instead of sending the puck into the attack zone ahead of Art, Bud made a whizzing slap shot from just beyond the center line. It blurred through the attack zone and bulged out the back of the goal net.

The stands erupted in a yell. The Viking goalie, who had left himself wide open while watching Art, stood stupefied.

The roar of the crowd was deafening. Bud couldn't hear the voices of his teammates crowding around him. It was one of the longest goal shots he had ever attempted.

The scoreboard changed: Battlers 3, Vikings 3.

"One to go!" Bud shouted, but no one could hear him in the din filling the arena. He held up one finger of his glove, and the Battlers nodded and skated swiftly into position for the next face-off. The Vikings looked grim.

The referee dropped the puck. Lou and the Viking center skirmished over it; the Viking got it out to his right wingman, who took it over the blue line into the Battler defense zone. Rod Stevens battled him along the boards, filched the puck from him, and shot it over the red line to the end boards.

Dupuis streaked around behind the net, and Lou moved up to help the goalie cover the undefended side of the zone. Dupuis dug the puck out, gave it to Rod, and swung back to guard the front of the net with the goalie. Lou moved down the ice and got the puck from Rod. Lou, about to be hip checked, sent the puck across to Peewee. The Viking forward playing Dupuis closed in determinedly, but the French Canadian didn't try to go down the right lane. He stickhandled toward the middle of the rink. The Viking forward closed in to forecheck. Peewee swerved away, farther across the rink. The Viking was determined to block him.

Suddenly Rod Stevens came between them and collided hard with the Viking forward. The referee's whistle shrilled, and he crossed his arms over his chest, signaling interference. "Two minutes," he told Rod.

Rod glanced contritely toward Bud as he skated past him. "Sorry," he said. "Just got too anxious."

As Rod and the referee skated to the penalty box, there was scrambling activity at both team benches. The Vikings were pulling out their two defensemen and the center to replace them with sharpshooting forwards. The Battlers pulled out Art Schoen and Lou Huff for two husky defensemen good at killing penalties.

The referee made the face-off where play had stopped. Bud, standing in for the face-off, ignored all actions of his opponent's stick and watched the referee's hand. He got the puck, but a jolting blow lifted his stick, and his opponent knocked the puck between Bud's skates. Before Bud could kick it clear, a stick blade came in from behind and hooked the rubber out into Viking possession. The Battlers raced into position for defense of the goal. The five Viking forwards came at them like a cavalry charge.

"Hold the box!" Bud yelled. "Hold the box!"

The Battler defense repulsed the onslaught. Dupuis growled something in French as the Vikings drove in again, and somehow he got the puck and shot it into clear ice. The temptation to go after it was resisted.

"Hold the box!" Bud shouted again.

A Viking shot the puck around behind the net. Palmer, the Battler goalie, didn't make the mistake of turning his whole body; he moved only his head, just far enough to watch the puck from the corner of his eye. Bud moved in beside a goalpost to help protect against a sudden angle shot as the puck came out from behind the red line.

A Viking deflected the puck across the rink, and another Viking forward wrist shot powerfully, right through the box defense. The puck struck Palmer's big stick—and the blade snapped! Half of it dangled, held only by the tape. There were gasps from the stands.

The rules about broken or damaged equipment were explicit. Any other player would have had to discard the broken stick immediately, tossing it out of the play to the boards, being certain he did not throw it at the puck or another player. He could play without a stick or go to his bench for a new one.

Palmer, as goalie, had three choices. He could continue to play with the broken stick, go for a new one while a defenseman tried to cover the goal for him, or wait for one of his teammates to bring him a new stick. No one from the bench could do it. Only someone on the ice, *leaving* the action, could replace the stick.

But the Battlers were already one man short. No one dared leave for even a moment. They desperately tried to freeze the puck or shoot it down the rink to slow the play, but the Vikings kept possession and began an intensified attack, seeking another opening to the goal.

It was a raging, swirling struggle. Skates rasped on ice. Sticks clashed like gunshots. A yelling bedlam filled the arena. In the midst of the melee, a momentary vision of a wagon train under Indian attack flashed before Bud's eyes.

Palmer fought back heroically as the puck blasted at the goal again and again. He deflected it with the pads, his body, the glove. He blocked another shot with a split that got his skate in front of the puck just in time. A flashing stick flipped the rebound; the puck hit the middle of the broken blade and was deflected into the net. The red light came on. Vikings, 4–3.

The Boise fans groaned.

Bud spoke breathlessly to Palmer. "Nice try," he gasped. "Great time for that stick to get broken." He held out his gloved hand. "I'll get you another one."

On the way to the bench, Bud glanced at the dangling part of the blade. Only about half the wood had jagged splinters. The rest must have been knocked off in the wild defense action and—

Then Bud stopped skating and just coasted, looking closer at the broken blade. Part of the break was too clean—no splinters. He examined the other section of the stick. Also clean. There were no splinters where it matched the broken-off part of the blade.

It could mean only one thing: Someone had sawed halfway through that blade and carefully concealed the cut with tape!

Dupuis skated to Bud. *"Qu'est-ce que c'est?"*

Bud showed him the goalie's stick. *"Le diable!"* Dupuis exclaimed angrily.

Tierney barked from the bench. "Hurry it up

out there! You trying to pull a penalty for delay of game?"

They skated quickly to the bench. Dupuis got a new stick for Palmer; Bud handed the broken one to the coach.

"Save that!" Bud snapped. "Don't let it out of your sight."

The coach looked down at the stick, and several other club members leaned for a close look. As Bud turned away, he saw their eyes widening. There hadn't been time for him to do it quietly. Now everybody knew: Someone on the club had helped to rig this game for the Battlers to lose.

Bud glanced at the clock and skated grimly to position for the face-off. There was barely enough time left to prevent the plot from being completely successful.

7
Washout

THE PUCK WAS DROPPED. The Vikings, leading, had the momentum. They got the puck and took it into the Battler defense zone. There was a wild scramble, and Dupuis, by sheer angry strength, got it back to neutral ice. The Vikings recovered, and again Dupuis, practically single-handedly, broke up the attack. Bud got the puck in neutral ice and took it into the attack zone. He got a hard hip check, and when he got his skates back under him, he saw the Vikings taking off down the rink again. Dupuis backskated, guarding his man. As the puck neared the goal, he closed in to aid Palmer.

The Vikings kept the puck away from Dupuis with quick, short passes in the slot. It looked as though an attempt would come from there and Palmer leaned forward in his crouch. Dupuis moved nearer to him.

The Viking center passed toward his forward, who had eluded Rod Stevens. The puck hit the referee, who had been easing in to keep a closer eye on the action. The puck deflected from the ref's skate into the nets. Cheering erupted from the Viking fans in the stands, but the referee spread his arms down and waved them. Washout. No goal.

The Viking captain irately confronted the referee. "It touched the goalie—"

"It did not," the official declared. "No goal on a deflection entirely from me."

The Viking captain argued with him all the way to the semicircle crease by the penalty time-keeper. Any further argument when the referee was in that crease would call for a bench penalty on the Viking club. The captain turned away.

Bud called to the Battlers, "That breaks the momentum."

But the Vikings still had the lead. Another score would cinch the game for them in the remaining minutes. They sent a two-on-one attack past Rod Stevens; Palmer made a save and got the puck to Lou. Two Vikings badgered Lou, who passed to Dupuis. He refused to be cowed by two Vikings who sought to block him off. He got the puck back to Lou.

Bud, Lou, and Art went down the rink in a three-on-two attack. Art dropped back, and Lou left a drop pass for a trailer shot. Art shot for the goal. The Viking goalie dove to deflect the shot; Bud swooped by and tipped the puck into the net.

Tied score—and the horn sounded, ending the game.

"Well, at least we didn't lose it," Bud said to Dupuis as they skated from the ice. Yet, in a way, it was a washout, for there would be no money paid or received on bets. There was no way for Gleason, the police, or anyone else to discover who had counted most on the Battlers losing.

At least now there was a piece of hard evidence: the goalie's rigged stick.

In the dressing room, there was thick silence. Gleason, Tierney, Doc Taylor, assistant coaches and trainers, and the players ringed the room with grim, set expressions. The goalie's broken stick, like a courtroom exhibit, lay on a trainer's table. The press and TV men had been barred.

Gleason moved to the table with an expression suggesting that his oil wells had all run dry. He looked at the broken stick, then swept his gaze around.

"Well, what about it?" he barked. Silence. He glared. "Speak up," he snapped. "We can't leave this situation frozen. We've got to play referee and get this cleared up. If we don't, it'll be done for us, by the league and maybe by the police. And there'll be more than one head broken before the right one is found. We've got to dig out of this corner ourselves." Still silence. Gleason sighed. "All right, I guess the only way to get this cleared up is to tell you that something like this"—he gestured toward the stick—"has been suspected for some time. We were hoping it could be discovered and squelched quietly, so as not to disrupt—"

"We?" someone questioned. "Who's *we?*"

Gleason was careful to keep his eyes averted from Bud. "It doesn't matter who *we* is. The main thing is—"

"It sure does matter," someone else interrupted. "You've had somebody spying on us!"

"So what?" another voice demanded. "In Tex's spot, you'd have done the same thing to try to keep it quiet. Look at us now; each one of us is beginning to suspect the guys on either side."

Other voices joined in.

"I still want to know who's *we?*"

"That lets one or more guys out of it, narrows the field."

Gleason nodded. "That's a point, but I'd still prefer not to name—"

"Why not? What's the point of that?"

Bud spoke up. "I've been working on this with Tex."

For a moment there was silence. Eyes stared at Bud. Then someone laughed.

"That's one for the book! The guy who's already been all but named, booed by the fans, had his name in the papers because—"

"Because," Bud cut in, "I *know* something rotten has been going on. And for a long time. My father suspected it, too. That's why he died. I'm convinced he was killed."

Silence again, but before Bud could go on, Rod Stevens spoke up. "Don't blow your top,

Bud. Those rumors about your father have never been proved or disproved."

Bud nodded, then pointed toward the broken stick. *"There's* evidence that something has been going on."

"And," Gleason declared, "let's stay with that, now that we've broken the silence. Anyone care to own up to it?" he asked, smiling grimly at the absurdity of his question. "Anyone care to make an accusation or voice a suspicion?"

No one spoke. Bud became aware of several glances in his direction.

The silence was extremely uncomfortable, not just for Bud, but for everyone in the room. Everyone was suspecting someone else and knowing that, in turn, he was being suspected.

Gleason sighed. He looked around at the club. "I don't want to point a finger any more than any of you do. I might be wrong, and it would only create resentment. But we *must* get this ironed out, one way or another."

"Maybe we won't have to," suggested Remy. "Maybe it won't happen again, now that everyone knows and will be watching."

Doc Taylor shook his gray head. "That would leave everything hanging in the air. Wouldn't make for good team play." He turned to Gleason. "You've got to get to the bottom of this, Tex."

"Have you got a suggestion?" the owner retorted, angry with frustration.

"Yes. I imagine we all have some suspicions, founded and unfounded. Why don't we each visit you, privately, and voice whatever we may be thinking? You can keep track, and if there's a lot of suspicion or evidence about any person or persons—"

"All right." Gleason cut him off. He looked around. "Except for maybe one rotten apple, I've got a swell crop of players here, and I'm not going to tip over the barrel. I'm sorry it happened this way tonight. Is everyone agreeable to Doc's suggestion?"

Heads nodded and voices murmured.

"Wait a minute," Bud called. "This way might lead to a solution, but it has a bad angle, too. It puts everyone in the club under suspicion. I think we can clear a lot of guys with one simple question." He turned to Palmer. "When was the last time you put new tape on your stick?"

"Good question," Remy exclaimed. "Then we'll know about when it must have been cut and who might have had a chance to—"

"All right," Gleason said, stopping any further comments. He turned to the goalie. "When?"

"That's easy," Palmer replied. "I retaped it this morning, before practice."

Tierney scowled. "Then you wouldn't have had any reason to examine it before the game."

"No. It was new tape; looked just like what I'd put on."

"Wasn't it marked from stopping pucks in practice?" Bud asked.

Palmer shook his head. "Coach had me working without my stick for most of the practice."

Bud hadn't known that. He'd been practicing at the other goal that morning.

"Where was the stick while you were practicing without it?" Tierney asked.

"On top of the nets. No one could have taken it without being seen. That stick was within my reach from the time I taped it until I dressed and left after practice. I left here at nine fifteen this morning."

"That lets me off the hook," an alternate forward declared. "I left at ten after nine."

"I was with you, remember?" another player declared.

"So," Gleason said slowly, "we can assume the

stick was cut and re-taped sometime between nine fifteen A.M. and game time. That eliminates those who left before Palmer, unless they came back and somehow got into the locked dressing room."

Bud saw Tierney frowning at him. Then Chuck spoke.

"I left after Palmer, but Rod and Art were with me. You said good-bye to us, Bud."

A stab of apprehension went through Bud. Now he understood Tierney's frown. He, Bud, had been alone in the dressing room, retaping the bantams' sticks. He could tell by the eyes looking at him that others were remembering that.

"I was here alone," he admitted. "But I didn't have enough time to retape the bantams' sticks *and* strip the tape from Palmer's, saw it, and re-tape it. Anyway, how would I know that Palmer was going to replace Chuck in the game tonight?"

"You suggested it to me," Tierney said quietly.

Bud stood up angrily. "Are you implying—"

Dupuis cut in. "Take it easy, Bud."

"I'm not implying anything," Tierney declared. "Just stating a fact."

"All right," Bud countered, "but you were

already thinking of pulling Chuck when I—"

"Why?" Chuck demanded. "Why was I pulled out?"

"Because of the score," Tierney snapped. "You were looking at the clock more than at the puck."

"I was worried about my father," Chuck muttered resentfully.

"Or maybe," said a voice from the corner of the room, "you *wanted* to be pulled out."

"Are you suggesting that I had another reason for wanting Palmer in there?" Chuck demanded. "All right," he said angrily. "It's a fact that the goalie has the best opportunity of anyone to throw games, just by letting the puck slip by." He looked around defiantly. "I haven't been doing that. I'll admit that at times, such as tonight, I haven't been at my best. Now, who wants to try to prove it's been deliberate?"

"No one, Chuck," Bud said. "There are times when any of us can look bad. That's the nature of the game. And it's easy to misinterpret appearances—I know."

"What appearances?" Chuck demanded, then nodded. "Oh, I get it. My father. Heavy medical expenses. So you're thinking—" Before Bud could answer, Chuck went on. "Well, let me tell you what I'm thinking about *you*, especially after what's come out here tonight."

"Knock it off, Chuck," Gleason said.

"Why?" Chuck faced Bud. "You've been clever covering it up. Like that nice pep talk you gave us at intermission, before you got me out and got Palmer in with his rigged stick."

Dupuis stepped between them, confronting Chuck. "Bud playcd hard, tied the game, saved us from a loss."

"Sure," Chuck retorted. "To cover up, when he couldn't hide that stick of Palmer's."

Bud pushed Dupuis aside. "I could have hidden it easily if I'd wanted to. If I had tossed it to the boards, it would have been gathered up and thrown in with the trash. I didn't have to show it to Tierney."

"That could have been a cover-up, too. 'Look what I discovered,' says the big hero. Then no one would think that you'd done it. They'd look for someone else."

Tierney growled to Gleason, "This is getting out of hand, splitting the club apart." He glowered at Bud. "And you—"

"Are you going to start implying things about me again?"

"Call it that if you want to," the coach snapped. "You *were* in here alone after practice this morning, weren't you?"

"I've admitted that. But since we're tossing suspicions around so freely, it was *you* who told me I'd left the door unlocked. You could have been in here alone while I was with Tex."

Chuck joined in. "And what about after the bantams' practice, Bud?"

"Dupuis was with me," Bud retorted. Someone laughed. Bud went on angrily. "There were two janitors here, then Doc came in and was here until—"

"They all left," Doc Taylor said, "and I was here alone. So maybe *I*—"

"Break it up!" Gleason bellowed. "I was a fool to hope this could be done calmly. Hockey players! Of all the blasted, ornery, short-tempered—" He shook his head. "You're still my kind of people, with one exception. He'll be found, but not this way, not by pulling the club apart. So lay off. Not another word. Is that clear?"

Glaring, he walked to the door and faced around. The parentheses about his mouth arced stiffly into a grim smile. "It's not going to be easy, after what's happened here, but try . . . for yourselves, for the club. Don't waste that fighting among yourselves. Save it for the ice, huh?"

The door closed after him, and there was uncomfortable silence in the room. Then Tierney spoke, very quietly.

"I was going to call a practice for Monday and Tuesday. Forget it. Take tomorrow and those two days off. Do something different. Don't see or talk to anyone else on the club. See if we can cool down. Next practice Wednesday morning."

Players began to change out of their gear. The door burst open, and Sid Seidler, the syndicated sports columnist, strode in.

"What goes on around here? First the door is locked, then Gleason gives me a brush-off—"

"Which you don't need," Bud remarked, motioning behind his back to Dupuis. "You look as though you just stepped out of a men's store window."

"—and now," Seidler went on, "you guys act as though the gentle game of hockey has committed suicide and is ready for burial."

From the corner of his eye, Bud saw Dupuis casually drop a jersey over the broken blade of the stick on the trainer's table and then face around with folded arms, as though on guard duty at a national monument.

"Nothing special, Sid," grumbled Tierney. "They've just been getting my usual harangue about things I thought they should have done."

"I don't believe it," Seidler said.

"Game postmortem, that's all," said Doc Taylor. He smiled. "They nearly lost. Wouldn't you try to find out why?"

"Of course." Seidler looked around shrewdly. "And just what did you find out?"

"We won't know," said Bud, "until we read about it in your column."

Several of the players laughed. Seidler gave Bud a look. "I hope that's a compliment."

"It was if your column this morning was."

Bud and Seidler stared at one another for a moment. Then the reporter pulled a small leather notebook from his coat pocket and began moving among the other players, seeking comments on the evening's game.

Bud picked up the goalie's stick and started toward the door with it. Tierney grabbed his arm and asked quietly, "Just where do you think you're going with that?"

"I was taking it to Tex to be locked up." Bud held it out, with the blade dangling. "Or did you have other plans for the evidence?"

The coach's eyes were hard. "We'll both take it."

Bud draped a jersey over the blade before he and Tierney entered the corridor.

Tex Gleason was slouched back in his swivel chair, his boots up on the desk. He sighed and got up. The stick was put in his personal storage cabinet and the door locked. Tierney turned toward the corridor.

"Wait a minute, coach," Bud requested. He sought for words. "I don't quite know how to say this. First, I'm sorry for what happened. It's my fault. You'd asked me, Tex, to keep things quiet, not to voice or exhibit any suspicions."

Gleason waved an arm and let it drop heavily. "What else could you have done out on the ice? I would have been as surprised as you were. It was our first real break."

No one smiled at the unintentional pun.

"As you said," Bud continued, "this club is too good to be split apart." He hesitated, finding words even more difficult now. "I . . . if it would help to hold things together, since there's already a lot of suspicion pointing my way. . . . Well, it might pull the rest of the club together if you suspended me for the time being."

"What are you saying?" Gleason demanded.

"Let them think you've decided I'm guilty."

"That won't stop the fixed games," Gleason retorted.

"They'll probably stop, anyway, for a while, now that this is in the open," Bud said. "But with me out of it, maybe the guys will stop suspecting each other. They'll play as a team. Meanwhile, we'll still be trying to discover just who—"

Gleason cut in. "With no fixed games until this heat is off, what makes you think we'd have any more success than we've had?"

Bud sighed.

Gleason looked at Tierney. "What do you think, Al?"

The coach took a moment before he replied. "After some of the things I implied about Bud, his offer to be suspended jolts me . . . changes my thinking." Tierney took a deep breath. "I'll be honest. I've resented Bud from the time I came here. I was always overshadowed by his father."

"Dad had great respect for you," Bud said.

"After his death, when I came here," Tierney said to Gleason, "I saw how thick you were with Bud. I thought I was just a fill-in until you were ready to put Bud in as head coach."

"That's never even been mentioned, Al, between Bud and me. You haven't stood in a shadow. You've moved the club ahead from where Bart left it."

"Thanks, Tex. I just wish you and Bud had let me in from the start on what you were trying to discover. I don't know if I would have believed it at first. But now. . . ." He shook his head. "As head coach, I say we need Bud on the ice."

"Agreed," Gleason said crisply. "No suspension. Sit down, you two. Let's see if we can sift anything out of what went on in the dressing room."

They talked for an hour. Their hopeless conclusion was that anyone could look bad on the ice if his actions were viewed with suspicion. No one in the club was exempt, least of all the goalie.

"That's the obvious member of any club," Gleason sighed. "And with that in mind," he admitted, unlocking a desk drawer and removing a folder, "I had a credit bureau quietly investigate Chuck. That was after I offered him an interest-free loan, which he refused."

"Refused?" Tierney asked. "After all the heavy medical expenses he's had with his father?"

"So I put the credit bureau on the job," said Gleason. He touched the folder. "He's used his savings and insurance, even mortgaged the home. To all appearances, he's on thin ice. But the expenses he's had just about balance against the resources he's used," Tex sighed. "Somewhere, there's something about someone that's escaping our attention. We've got to find it before there's another fixed game. I'm going to have the bureau go to work on every member of the club. I'm also going up to see the league governor. I stalled him off this morning, but now I'd better go and throw a loop on him, before he throws one on me and the club. While I'm gone, you two see if you can get this club unsnarled."

Tierney grunted. "After what happened in the dressing room—"

Bud nodded. It was going to be very rough ice.

8
A Team Divided

WEDNESDAY MORNING PRACTICE was a disaster.

There wasn't the usual banter in the dressing room. Even Bud and Dupuis didn't talk much. The armed-truce silence was depressing. Bud surreptitiously tested the blade of his stick— solid. No one commented when Palmer chose a new stick with a number 12 lie and began taping the bare blade.

On the ice, Tierney started the entire club off with skating practice. The sound of the skates seemed like an ominous growl. Each man skated

143

alone; when two players brushed going around behind the nets or reversing to skate backward, there was a cold glance between them.

Tierney looked grim when he finally broke up the squad into groups for puck passing, goal shooting, and checking. It was touchy; everyone was playing too gingerly. Ordinarily, Tierney would have jawed at them, but they were like a pack of strange dogs, stiff-legged, hackles on end, waiting for a fight to start.

Art Schoen stickhandled down the boards, Dupuis skating backward in front of him. Art shifted his head to one side and spurted to get by in the other direction. Dupuis wasn't deked—he gave Art a hard hip check. The forward went down with a clatter of stick and skates. He was back on his blades in a flash, overtaking Dupuis, who was stickhandling before passing the puck to another forward. Art gave Dupuis an elbow in the back. Dupuis dropped his stick and whirled, pulling off his gloves and baring fists.

Bud and Tierney arrived quickly from opposite directions. The coach barked at Art.

"Go on around behind the nets and take your place in the line over there."

"Did you see the check he gave me?" Art

protested, glaring from Tierney to Dupuis.

"It was mild," Bud said over his shoulder while holding back Dupuis. "Nothing like you'd get in a game."

Peewee tried to push Bud aside. *"Non, mon ami*. Let me show him a *real* check!"

"Knock it off!" Tierney barked. "Both of you!"

The momentary silence was broken by a loud *whack-thump* out in the slot by the goal. Lou Huff had golf-clubbed a slap shot, which Chuck had blocked with his body. In spite of the pads, Chuck had a pained expression. He advanced from the crease.

"You trying to prove something, hotshot?"

"Whatsamatter, you got a guilty conscience?" Lou replied.

Chuck flung down his stick and tore off his gloves. Lou did the same. They closed in, fists flying. Rod Stevens moved in, apparently to separate them, but instead took some punches at Lou. Remy took Rod on, while Lou went at Chuck again. Players converged from all corners of the rink. Voices rose in shouts. Accusations flew. Sticks clashed. Fists flailed.

Bud, Tierney, and Dupuis waded in, trying to break it up, but didn't succeed until everyone else was exhausted or had spent his anger. One man was out cold. Others had bruised faces, blackening eyes, bleeding noses.

"Bud," Tierney snapped, "phone Doc Taylor to get over here." As Bud, breathing hard, skated from the ice, he heard the coach warning the club members: "Anyone starts this up again will be slapped with a hundred-dollar fine."

At the side of the rink were the two maintenance men who had played impromptu hockey the previous Saturday. One spoke to Bud.

"You see why I just stick to betting?"

Bud paused. "Stick around. I want to see you after I make a phone call." When Bud returned a moment later, he asked the janitor about the bet he had made on last Saturday's game.

"Nothing came of it. Tied score."

"I know," Bud said, "but who took your bet?" The man stared at him. Bud tried again. "It's important."

"Why? You trying to make trouble for someone?"

"Look," Bud said patiently, "I know gambling is illegal. I'm not trying to make trouble for you. Maybe you made the bet with a friend, someone you work with. If so, I'm not interested. But if it was with a stranger—and a good-sized bet—then maybe. . . ."

The janitor shrugged, looking at his partner. "It was only five bucks. What'd you expect on my pay and with four kids to feed?"

Tierney called a halt to further practice that day. When Bud had changed from his playing gear, he went to a pay phone and dialed, then broke off and got his dime back before he'd completed the call.

"Qu'est-ce que c'est?" Dupuis asked.

"Strickland said he had a big bet on Saturday's game," Bud explained. "I was going to ask his wife where to contact him, but it's too risky. I might have given her an inkling of what it was about, and she didn't know he was betting heavily. I'll find some excuse to see him alone some evening or speak to him alone Saturday morning. The way things went this morning, we're not going to get a line on anyone in the club, so maybe we've got to come at him from another direction."

Dupuis nodded. "Elbow in the back," he growled. "Wait till Art sees what he gets the next time I check him."

"Take it easy," Bud cautioned.

The whole club practiced with extreme caution on Thursday and Friday. Afterward, Tierney could only shake his head and scowl.

Gleason had returned to Boise from Canada that morning. Bud and Tierney were in his office.

"If they're going to be like that against Portland," Tierney informed him, "we might as well default."

"They'll snap out of it, I hope," Gleason said. He leaned against the desk. "I laid everything out to the league governor. He agreed with me it would look bad to suspend or fine our club at this time. That would give the whole league a black eye. He also agrees that the possibility of any more fixed games is slim for a while. He's giving us that much time to get this straightened out. But at the first hint of something going wrong again, he'll crack down on us."

"That's a big help," Tierney grumbled. "Nothing's going to happen to give us a lead, but we're still supposed to do something about it."

"He's not leaving it all in our lap," Gleason went on. "From his end, there'll be spotters in every crowd at our games. There will be quiet feelers to determine if organized gambling is involved—which it probably is."

"It's organized, all right," Bud declared. "Look how long it's been going on, with no clues, except for that broken stick—and whatever Dad discovered before he was killed."

"And *because* of what he discovered," Gleason reminded him grimly, "he died. Now I'm worried about you, Bud. Too many people know you're deeply involved in our investigation. You're not keeping anything from me, are you?"

Bud thought of his possibly getting a lead through Strickland, but that was just a guess. "I've told you everything," he said.

At bantam practice on Saturday morning, Bud got Mark's father aside.

"Wayne, I know this is none of my business, but I'd like to ask you something about that big bet you said you had on the game last week."

Strickland darted a glance toward his wife, sitting a short distance away in the stands.

"Nothing came of it," he said nervously. "The score was tied."

Bud nodded. "I know, but the bet interests me. I—"

Strickland leaned closer. "I shouldn't have

told you about it. I certainly hope you've kept it to yourself. You could place me in a very embarrassing position."

"That's not my intention," Bud assured him. "I'm only asking because you hinted that it was a good-sized bet."

There was worry on Strickland's face and in his voice. "Forget it, please. Can't you understand? I shouldn't have bet so heavily—fortunately, I didn't lose it—and I'm not going to do it again. I used my own money, of course, but if anyone knew that a bank employee—"

"What I want to know, Wayne," Bud cut in, "won't involve you in any way. I understand your position. All I want to know is *who* you made the big bet with."

Strickland stared at him, then gave a short laugh. "Won't involve me in any way! Huh! I don't know what you're after, Carson, but I can't help you. Sorry." He turned away and moved along the stands to rejoin his wife.

That night, the Battlers took to the ice against the Portland Pumas and got mauled. They didn't make a single goal; the Pumas socked three into the nets. The Boise fans booed as the club left the rink, a team that had beaten itself.

"I felt like booing, too," Tierney snapped in the dressing room. "Of all the unglued plays, sloppy passing, lousy checking—"

He practiced them hard every day, trying to restore their edge, but the only edge evident was in individual attitudes toward one another. Two more practice fights occurred that week, and hundred-dollar fines were levied on the participants. On Friday, the club flew to Utah. The Salt Lake Seagulls rubbed salt in the Battlers' wounds, 4–1. The only Battler goal was made by Rod Stevens. It was one of the few times that the Battlers even got into the attack zone. He stole the puck from a Seagull forward, saw an opening, and made a long shot that streaked past the goalie.

At bantam practice on the following Saturday, in an intrasquad game, Mark Strickland netted the winning goal for his team. His proud parents gushed over him.

"If he keeps on improving this way," Bud said with a smile, "maybe we ought to option him now, so the Battlers will be sure to get him when he's eighteen."

"Attaboy!" Strickland exclaimed to his son.

"Now you're really on your way!"

Mark's face glowed. "Wait till Uncle Ed hears! I told him you were going to make me a player like you."

"Don't copy me. Be yourself," Bud said. He added wryly, "Anyway, I'm not doing too well lately."

"You'll win again!" Mark said confidently. "Uncle Ed says you will. He—"

"Mark," his father interrupted, "come over and get your windbreaker on. You're all sweaty. You'll get a chill."

Mrs. Strickland smiled at Bud. "Mark's Uncle Ed is my brother. He's quite a hockey fan. He'd be playing, if his leg hadn't been crippled in an automobile accident. He rarely misses a Battler game."

"Even in Canada," Mark declared.

"Mark," his father said curtly, "your windbreaker. Come on," he said to his wife, "or we'll be late."

"For what?" she inquired.

Wayne Strickland didn't answer. He moved away, reaching over the boards to motion Mark toward a gate. He began to scold Mark and didn't glance back.

Bud skated away slowly. Mark's Uncle Ed—was he the man with whom Strickland had made his bet? Was he the man who had been beside Mark during the Viking game? If Uncle Ed was such a Battler fan, why had he looked almost pleased when the Battlers were losing?

Dupuis joined Bud on the rubber mat leading to the dressing room.

"You should be smiling. Your protégé scored."

"I think Mark really did score for me," Bud murmured.

Bud got to the rink early that night for the game with the Ottawa Otters. In the owner's office, he told Gleason about Mark's Uncle Ed.

"There may not be anything to it," Bud concluded, "but—"

Gleason nodded. "But we've got to clutch at anything. I'll have him investigated. If anything comes up, I'll sic the police on him." Gleason didn't look too hopeful. "Probably just a family bet, though." He motioned to a newspaper on his desk. "The sportswriters are lambasting us. How does it look for tonight?"

"Depressing," Bud answered. "We really need some kind of break to pull the club out of its doldrums. Morale couldn't be worse."

In the dressing room, between warm-up and the start of the game, the players acted as though they had already lost the game.

Tierney glowered at them. "You guys have gotten pretty good at fighting among yourselves. Now, how about the guys on the other team?" Glaring around, he pointed at various players who had been in fights during practice. "So you still got chips on your shoulders because one of us is a rat and you don't want to be called *it*. All right, let me tell you something: The word's out about our problem. Everybody's talking about it. Those guys out on the ice tonight think we'll be pushovers because of it. And they're probably right, too." Tierney paused. "But when you cover a man tonight, look at his face. Look in his eyes. You know what he's thinking? He's thinking: 'I wonder if this is the guy who's blowing it for the Battlers.' That's what he's thinking! And when you miss a check or make a lousy pass, that guy'll smile and think, 'Yep, he's the one.' The Otter you're covering is the one who suspects you!"

When the game started it looked like another debacle for the Battlers. Then Art Schoen got roughly boarded by an Ottawa defenseman. Art slashed with his stick; the Otter ducked, spread his hands apart on his own stick, and rammed it with a cross-check high on Art's chest. Art was slammed back hard against the boards. The referee's whistle shrilled.

Rod Stevens, skating up fast, collided with the Ottawa center, who was also approaching the scene. Each mistook the collision for antagonism. Sticks went down, gloves came off, fists formed. Bud, skating across to help the referee and linesman break it up, was tripped from behind by a stick. Dupuis immediately cuffed the man who had tripped Bud.

The Battlers' long pent-up resentments erupted. Fights broke out all over the rink. Spectators in the stands roared, reminiscent of the days of Rome and gladiators battling in the Coliseum.

The referee, linesmen, Bud, and a few other players finally got it all stopped.

It was just a temporary pause. Blood had been drawn. Antagonisms were aroused. The game resumed, with several penalties imposed. There were more fights, more penalties. The first period ended with no score, unless you counted black eyes, cuts, and bruises.

In the second period, everyone coasted, getting a breather, and it ended with still no score.

In the third period, both teams tried harder to score, and it became a gladiators' arena again. The penalty timekeeper was overworked; so were the teams' doctors and trainers. With time-outs called by the referee to break up fights and impose penalties, the twenty-minute period lasted nearly an hour. And when the final buzzer sounded, the score was 0–0.

Sid Seidler's next column called the Boise rink the Bucket of Blood. He compared the game to a meeting of two rival street gangs who sought to wipe each other out. The *Boise Statesman* published an editorial deploring the unsportsmanlike behavior of the teams whose respective countries, Canada and the United States, shared three thousand miles of border.

On Monday evening, Mark Strickland's father telephoned Bud. "I'm calling to let you know that Mark is withdrawing from the bantams."

"I'm sorry to hear that," Bud replied. "He was coming along so—"

"I don't want my boy to be involved in anything like what went on Saturday."

"Wait a minute, Mr. Strickland," Bud said.

"I'll admit that last Saturday night's game was wild—"

"That's putting it mildly."

"Nevertheless, Mr. Strickland, you've seen such occurrences before. Maybe not on such a scale, but those things do happen in a game like ice hockey. I recall your once remarking that it was like viewing two sports for the price of one: hockey and fighting. So I don't understand why now—"

"I've stated my reason."

Bud's eyes narrowed. "Are you sure you've given me the real reason, Mr. Strickland?"

"I don't know what you're talking a—"

"I'm thinking of our recent conversation about your bet."

There was a click; then Bud heard the dial tone. Strickland had hung up.

Bud telephoned Gleason and told him about Strickland. "I think there might be an angle with the brother-in-law."

"It sounds like a possibility," Gleason agreed. "I'll tell my boys to really dig. But there's something to it I don't like. My guess is that if the brother-in-law is involved, he's learned that you're getting close. He's probably put some pressure on Strickland to shut the door. Maybe that's why the kid is being pulled out of the bantams."

"That's my thought, too," said Bud.

"Don't let your guard down for a minute, Bud. Your father may have made that mistake."

Bud pulled back a curtain and looked at the lighted cross up on Table Rock, near where his father had died.

"I'll keep my eyes open," he promised.

"Good. I've also asked Dupuis to keep an eye on you," Gleason said.

At breakfast the next morning, when Bud started to get up from the table, Dupuis's heavy hand pushed him back down into the chair.

"*Non,* finish your breakfast first."

Bud stared at him. "I had three eggs, five strips of bacon, four slices of toast. What more—"

"Finish your milk."

"What's this all about?" Bud grinned.

"Tex said I was to take care of you. I take care."

"He didn't mean—"

"Finish your milk," Peewee insisted sternly, though there was a slight gleam in his eye.

Bud turned to his sister. "Put an apron on him. A real frilly one."

"She may if she wishes," Dupuis said, "but you will still finish your milk."

"Who's going to make me?" Bud demanded.

"*We* are," said his sister. "You're not going to have a fight over it. That's my new china." She looked at the adhesive on Bud's forehead, the bruises on his face. "Wasn't there enough fighting last Saturday night?" She put her hand on Dupuis's shoulder. "It makes me feel so good to know you're standing by Bud."

"*Merci.*" Dupuis smiled at her, then glowered at Bud. "Finish your milk."

That afternoon, the battered Battlers boarded a chartered plane for a flight to Regina, Saskatchewan. The following night, they played the Regals. Though they had vented a lot of their pent-up anger against the Otters, the Battlers were still divided among themselves. The Regals took them easily, 4–2.

Tierney sat with Bud and Dupuis as their plane flew eastward to Montreal.

"If this keeps on," he muttered, "we won't last another season. I almost wish we'd crash, so we could default the rest of our games."

Dupuis signaled the stewardess, then motioned to Bud.

"Bring him some milk, *s'il vous plait.*"

Bud spoke to Tierney. "Maybe, when we get home, Tex will have some good word."

"There's only one good word I want to hear," Tierney said. "It's *win.*"

9
Shale Ice

Montreal had long been the capital city of ice hockey. Despite the late hour when the Battlers' plane landed, there was a sizable crowd at the airport, displaying homemade signs and chanting that *Les Maréchals,* their beloved Marshals, would massacre the Battlers.

There were a few scattered cheers for the Boise club, probably from U.S. citizens who lived and worked in Montreal or had crossed the border from New York and the New England states. Bud searched among their faces in the crowd but failed to spot Mark Strickland's uncle.

Beside him, Peewee let out a joyous shout and charged to meet his mother, father, sisters, brothers, uncles, aunts, cousins, and friends with tight hugs. There were also warm greetings from the relatives for Bud, who had met most of them on other occasions. Peewee's youngest brother, Jean, clung to Bud's hand, then looked worried as Bud put on a scowl and pointed to a gold *Les Maréchals* pin.

"I forgot. I will not wear it when you play them."

"Okay." Bud grinned. "Then I'll play on *your* team on the lake tomorrow morning."

Jean's face beamed. Bud turned and called to Tierney as the club moved toward a bus that would take them to their hotel.

"See you at practice tomorrow afternoon."

"One o'clock sharp," Tierney reminded him.

Bud and Dupuis rode with the family to their home out on *Côte des Neiges* Road. A big meal awaited them. There was constant chatter, then quieter conversation after the younger family members were sent off to bed. Peewee's oldest brother, René, became thoughtful.

"Is there anything to the rumors I've been

hearing and reading about?" he asked.

"Plenty," Bud replied. He gestured toward a French-language newspaper, spotting Sid Seidler's name. "Has he had something more to say about us?"

"*Oui.* He discounts rumors about some games you have lost, saying no one would have to fix a game the way your club has been playing."

Peewee nodded. "That is our big problem. There will be no more fixed games until we start winning again."

"There's still the angle Tex is working on," Bud said, wishing he could sound more hopeful. "Maybe you can help, René. There's an American who attends a lot of our games in Canada. We think he bets heavily. If you spot him, let us know." Bud described Mark Strickland's uncle.

After a few hours' sleep young Jean awakened Bud and Dupuis. "*Allons-y!*"

Peewee opened one eye and growled.

"You promised last night you would go to the lake." Jean prodded at his big brother's bulky shape. "I know. You're afraid Bud and my team will beat you."

Dupuis flung back the covers and reared up

in the bed. *"Sacre-bleu!* I will grind you into the ice for that."

"Yaaah!" Jean retorted, ducking the pillow thrown at him.

It was great to play outdoors. The crisp air felt as though it were scouring lungs that had breathed too much city smog. The blue sky looked enameled; around the edges of the lake, the snow was unsullied by grime and dust.

The kids weren't cowed by the huge figures of Bud and Dupuis playing on opposing teams. The youngsters drove right at them, poke checking, hip checking, shoulder checking. Bud and Peewee let themselves be tumbled to the ice.

"Allons-y!" Jean yelled when he got the puck.

Dupuis skated backward before him; they looked like David and Goliath. Jean avoided a hip check, swept around his big brother, and shot the puck into the net.

Dupuis gaped at Bud. *"Whew!* I really tried to stop him!"

"You're getting old, Peewee," Bud chuckled.

A few moments later, as Bud stickhandled down the outdoor rink, Dupuis shouted, "I will take him! I will show him who is old!"

Just at the moment Dupuis swung to hip

check, Bud felt his skate break through some
shale ice, thin ice that had a hollow layer beneath
it. He plunged forward. The blade of his stick
slipped under one of Dupuis's skates, and the
butt end swung up, propelled by Bud's plunging
body. The hickory smashed into Peewee's head.
Bud and the big French Canadian crashed to the
ice. The kids yelled, seeing both men go down
hard.

"Sorry, Peewee." Bud smiled. "I didn't—"

He saw flowing blood. Peewee lay very still.
Bud tore off his gloves.

"Get me some snow!"

He dug under his sweater for a handkerchief,
filled it with snow, and held it against Dupuis's
head. Dupuis came to quickly. When he saw the
worried faces of all the kids, he smiled.

"It is nothing. I have had worse."

He started to sit up. His face contorted with
pain, and his hand went toward his right shoulder, as if to protect it.

"Let me help you," Bud said.

"It is nothing," said Peewee. "A little—a little
exercise and. . . ."

But the shoulder was already swelling badly.
Bud phoned the hotel where the Battlers were

staying, then he and René Dupuis drove Peewee into town.

Doc Taylor pursed his lips after examining Dupuis. "Shoulder separation. Not as bad as I expected, but he won't play against the Marshals tonight."

"That's great!" Tierney growled, scowling at Bud. "Couldn't you guys have been careful?"

"It was an accident . . . shale ice."

At the afternoon news briefing, Tierney tried to minimize the accident, saying he was confident Dupuis would be in to help defend against the powerful Marshals. Sid Seidler, who was in Montreal to cover this game and an NHL game the next night, lingered after the other writers had gone.

"Too bad it wasn't someone else," he said to Bud. "I mean, any two others beside you and Dupuis."

"What are you driving at?" Bud asked.

Seidler looked around before he answered. "I won't put it in my column. But in light of the rumors about you, Bud, the fact that you accidentally disabled a key player—"

Bud felt anger surging. "Didn't you say in your

column yesterday that we didn't have to *do* anything to lose games?"

"Yes, that's right. I did. Sorry I brought up
the subject. Good luck, Bud."

Tex Gleason came in and nodded toward another room. Bud and Tierney followed.

"Just got a phoned report from Boise about
Strickland's brother-in-law. His name is Halloway, Ed Halloway. Canadian, born in Edmon-
ton. He's assistant sales manager of a big barber
and beauty shop supply company. Has to travel
around a lot in the U.S. and Canada. He gambled
heavily and got into a bad jam in Las Vegas but
got out of it somehow."

"Then it *is* organized gambling," Bud said.

Gleason frowned, shaking his head slightly.
"My boys dug hard on that and couldn't find any
link. In fact, the organized people are rather re-
sentful, now that they've learned about him. My
boys think that someone bailed him out of his
jam."

"And so," Tierney surmised, "he's paying for
it by helping to fix games."

"Very likely. My boys tabbed it that he takes
a lot of bets. Big ones; nothing less than three
figures. Yet he doesn't show it when he collects.

He's either handing it over to someone else or banking it under fictitious names." Gleason paused, then went on pointedly. "He's here. In Montreal."

Tierney broke his silence with a sharp snort. "What for? He doesn't have to fix this game! Who'd be betting on us, anyway? There's only a handful of people here who would back us."

"Where is he?" Bud asked. "Are you keeping an eye on him?"

Gleason shook his head. "Not yet. I'll skip the details of how the boys found out he's in town. He's using an assumed name, and, as usual, he's disguised—"

"Sure, that fits," Bud exclaimed. "You said he works for a barber and beauty supply company. He must be stocked with wigs and toupees for men."

"That's probably why we never found the red-head who heckled you," Gleason said. "He could have slipped into a men's room and changed the wig for hair of a different color." Gleason sighed. "If we'd only had this information sooner. . . ." He glanced at Bud. "Guess my end of it hit shale ice, too."

Tierney shrugged helplessly. "Just the breaks.

From where I stand, we've got nothing to worry about except how much we're going to lose by tonight."

Gleason gave him a sharp look. "You're not going to convey that attitude to the club, are you?"

"Of course not. Come on, Bud. Give me a hand. Let's see if we can get them jumping."

When the Battlers appeared on the ice for their warm-up, the Dupuis clan and a few others made enough noise to offset what they lacked in numbers. Bud saw his teammates smile or grin. It was always a tough psychological factor to play away from home with little or no rooting from the stands. But with Peewee leading, his arm in a sling, the little group gave the Battlers a lift. They were drowned out by cheers from the rest of the spectators when the mighty Marshals came out, however.

In the dressing room after the warm-up, when the buzzer gave the three-minute warning for the start of the game, Tierney kept his remarks brief.

"We're going out against a tough outfit, but we're not the only ones who are facing it tonight. It's just as tough, and takes the same kind of guts, for Peewee's family to sit out there, among friends, and cheer us against their hometown team. Let's give them something to cheer about!"

Lou Huff got the puck on the face-off. The Marshals regained it when their goalie caught a shot from Bud and tossed the puck aside. The Montreal contingent knew that the absence of Dupuis would weaken the right side of the Battlers' defense. Whenever they got the puck, they attacked that area. At 17:02 of the first period, they harried the Battler defense out of position and slammed the puck into the nets.

Tierney substituted a new man on the Battlers' right defense. Lou Huff and Bud did their best to help fight off attacks in that zone. Then, after a quick pass, the Marshals attacked from the other side, scoring again at 19:50. With such a short time remaining, the referee, with the agreement of both captains, ended the period. The ten seconds remaining would be added to the second period.

In the dressing room, Tierney confined his remarks mainly to defense. "Don't defend so far out. They're getting by too easily. Stay closer to the crease. We'll regain the puck there."

The tightened defense blunted the Marshals'

attack. Bud spotted an opportunity it presented the Battlers for a special play. When Tierney pulled him out for a breather, Bud explained it to the coach.

"Good," Tierney agreed. He sent in a substitute for Art Schoen when the puck was out of the Battler defense zone. Art listened to Tierney's instructions and nodded. The coach signaled the alternate forwards to come off the ice at the first safe opportunity. It came when the referee whistled for a face-off as Chuck smothered the puck in the crease.

"Go to it," Tierney snapped.

As the alternate forwards came through the gate, Bud and Art went out onto the ice. At the face-off in the Battler defense zone, the Marshals got the puck. As expected, they took it to the weak side of the defense, faked, and fired the puck suddenly at the goal. Chuck went down in a split. Rod Stevens was supposed to get the puck away from the front of the net; instead, he swept the rebound to Lou Huff. It was intercepted.

Bud swooped in to poke check and took the puck into neutral ice. The Marshal defense raced to get between him and the goal. Bud sped, stick-handling across the blue line into the attack zone. His skates shaved ice, and to his surprise, he avoided the hip check. Tilting his blade, Bud wrist shot. The goalie rapped his stick on the ice in frustration as the puck streaked into the far corner. The red light came on, and the Dupuis cheering section yelled their heads off.

Montreal 2, Boise 1.

Bud swung past Art Schoen. "If they get the puck into our defense zone—"

"I heard Tierney," Art retorted.

Bud sighed. The Battlers were still unglued. It wasn't just Art; none of them even displayed the usual exuberance over a goal.

The Marshal center won the draw. When the puck couldn't be regained in neutral ice, the Battler defense quickly tightened about the crease. A Marshal forward had the puck. Unimpeded because the Battler defense wasn't playing man-to-man, he mistook the screams of Montreal fans for encouragement rather than warning. Bud was speeding down the ice behind him.

Bud stole the puck with a quick poke check and streaked down the rink. He swept it across the blue line. Lou Huff's stick caught it and kept it moving forward. He faked a pass back to Bud but backhanded to Art. The Battler forward got it in past the goalie with a sizzling shot.

Tied score.

Three and a half minutes later, Art Schoen
stole the puck from the Marshal forward on his
side of the rink. The forward whirled, lunged
after Art, and hooked his blade on Art's waist.
The referee whistled and signaled the penalty.

Tierney pulled out his two defensemen and
sent in two forwards to take advantage of the
Montrealers being one man short. The Battlers
got the puck and went down the rink in a power
play, but the Marshal defense was impregnable.
They wouldn't break formation to give any
opening.

The two-minute penalty was almost up, when
a shot by Lou was deflected, skittering in front
of Bud. Bud shot his stick straight forward, like
a billiard cue. He heard a whistle and yelling
from the stands, then saw the staring face of the
defenseman and the disbelieving expression of
the goalie. The puck was barely over the red line
between the goal posts. The Battlers were ahead,
3–2!

"Man!" Art Schoen exclaimed. "Tierney ought
to have pool tables on the rink for practice!"

Lou Huff slapped Bud's arm. Rod Stevens

grinned. Bud heard Peewee cheer.

The face-off. Bud felt that the Battlers were becoming a team again. But the mighty Marshals, back to full strength, *were* one. They furiously attacked the Battler goal. The Battler defense held off a score, but there was no opportunity for the forward line, Bud, Lou, and Art, to launch an attack of their own. Nor was there opportunity, under continuous Montreal attack, for the defense line to be relieved with substitutions. At 18:35 the Marshals tied the score 3–3.

Dupuis came down to the dressing room after the second period ended.

"*Magnifique!* My throat feels like my shoulder. I did not expect to cheer so much."

Bud nodded, frowning.

Peewee peered at him. "Why are you not smiling?"

Bud didn't answer then, but just before Dupuis went back to the stands, Bud drew him to one side. "I may be wrong, but there's something I want you to watch for."

Bud spoke softly. Dupuis listened, and his expression became a deepening scowl. "You really think so?"

"If he's doing what I think he is," Bud muttered, "he'll have to do it again in this final period. So keep your eye on *him* instead of the puck . . . at all times."

Dupuis whispered, "You have told this to Tierney and Gleason?"

"Not yet. Not until I'm sure of it."

Tierney and Gleason had other matters to occupy their attention. The coach had his club in the midst of a tough game. The owner was trying to find Strickland's brother-in-law, Ed Halloway. Bud wasn't certain about the thing he had become aware of in the first and second periods. It was hard to pin down anything in the fast game of ice hockey, but maybe with Dupuis watching from the stands. . . .

When the third period began, the Battlers had some semblance of their old teamwork. But the Marshals, leading the league in points toward the end-of-season play-offs, were determined not to have their rating lowered, especially not by a club that had been in the midst of a bad losing streak.

In the first seven minutes, the Marshals ran the game their way, nearly scoring three times. Then the Battlers shifted the action toward the other goal. The Marshals halted it, reversed it. Heavy

pressure brought the puck inside the crease, barely an inch from the red line, when Chuck
dropped on it so heavily that he snapped a thrust-
ing Marshal stick.

Fifteen minutes of the period were gone before the Battlers were able to break the puck
loose from their defense zone more than momen-
tarily. Bud, Lou, and Art moved the attack down
the rink, closely covered by a determined Marshal
defense line. The puck went from Lou to Art,
back to Lou, back to Art again, before they penetrated the attack zone.

Art left a drop pass for Rod Stevens, who sped
the puck to Lou. Lou, faking to deke the goalie,
zipped the puck sideways to Bud.

With blade tilted to cup the puck, Bud's
sweeping stick deflected the pass into the net!

A loud moan rose from the throats of Montreal fans in the stands, but it failed to smother
the yelps, yells, and screams from the Dupuis
section.

Bud looked up at that section of seats but
failed to spot Peewee. Darn it! He'd told him
what to watch for in this period. If he'd missed
spotting it. . . .

"Bud! Bud!" Art Schoen was calling urgently.

The referee and centers were in the neutral ice circle, and other players were in position for the face-off. Bud thrust with his skates to get near his Marshal defenseman and prevent a Montreal play in that direction. The puck dropped; the Marshals got it.

"Defense! Defense!" Tierney bellowed from the bench.

When the final buzzer sounded, it was Battlers 4, Marshals 3.

The Battlers crowded around Tierney and danced on their skates, raising their sticks triumphantly. It was great to taste victory again. Bud smiled, but inwardly he was disturbed. There was something he had to tell Tierney, but not now. Why spoil the exultation?

Bud smiled and nodded as the club's rejoicing continued in the dressing room. He skinned out of his jersey and the pads underneath and unlaced his boots. No shower now—he had something else on his mind, something he must do. But where the devil was Dupuis?

Bud was stabbing into his street clothes, when Sid Seidler and several other sportswriters came in.

"Well, surprise!" Sid exclaimed. "Surprise!"

"It sure was." Bud nodded. He couldn't speak to Tierney now. It would draw too much attention if he tried to get the coach to one side.

"See you later, Al," Bud called as he went into the corridor and nearly collided with Dupuis.

"Where have you—"

"I saw it!" Dupuis interrupted, nodding his head vigorously. *"Oui!* I watch like you say, and I see it! Oh, how I see it!"

"Good," Bud said eagerly. "Then you know."

The door behind him opened, striking his shoulders.

Dupuis, turning away, was pulling Bud along. "We go. I was just coming to get you. He is leaving. We must follow. Hurry. *Vite!"*

They ran, pushing, through fans leaving the rink, Bud leading because of Peewee's bad shoulder, Peewee calling directions right behind him. Dupuis's hand clutched Bud as they reached the parking lot.

"Le voilà!" He pointed through swirling snow.

They slowed, watching a man about twenty feet ahead. They paused by a large car to watch.

"He's getting into that yellow sedan," Bud murmured. He glanced quickly about. "If we only had a car to follow—"

"Here." Dupuis thrust keys into Bud's hand. "I borrowed from René, just in case. Go get it. Red hardtop. Next row."

Bud ran. Dupuis followed more slowly, looking over the tops of parked cars toward the yellow car.

Bud found René's car, started up the engine and windshield wipers, and backed out. A few cars away, someone else was backing out and would block him. Dupuis dashed forward, swept snow from the rear window of that car, and pounded on the glass.

"Non! Non! Non!" he roared, leaning against the car as though to push it back out of the way. The car stopped with a jolt. Bud stopped behind it to let Dupuis get in. He saw startled, frightened faces peering from the other car.

"You scared the devil out of them, you big lug!"

Dupuis turned. *"Pardon! Merci!"* he called grinning, but he received no smiles of acknowledgment. He faced forward grimly as Bud swung into the street.

"Le voilà!" Dupuis pointed to the yellow car half a block ahead.

Bud stayed just close enough to keep the car

in sight through the falling snow. "Where were you during the third period?" he asked Dupuis. "I didn't see you with your family."

"*Non*. I moved to the end, behind the Marshal goal, to watch better. You were right. That Montreal defense—he was smooth, but I know he deliberately screened his goalie from your winning shot."

Bud nodded, turning a corner, skidding on the snowy pavement. "And if you think back to the first and second periods, I'm sure he let some of my shots get by—some that he could have blocked or checked."

"We were caught off guard," Dupuis said. "We were watching for a loss but it was fixed for us to *win*. We were tricked."

"We sure were," Bud agreed, keeping his eyes on the snowy tracks of the yellow car. "But we're wise to two of them now. Maybe this will put a stop to fixed games once and for all." He frowned. "Do you see where he's leading us?"

"Mont Royale," Dupuis said. "Almost like—"

Bud finished for him. "Like Table Rock back in Boise, where my father died.

"There's probably a payoff for what he did in the game tonight," Bud said. The thought made him glance in the rearview mirror. Snow coated the rear window, but there was a bit of glow coming through it. "Peewee, that means he'll be meeting someone up here. I think there's a car behind me. Lean out your window and see."

"*Oui,* another car behind us, coming fast. Catching up."

Bud pressed down on the throttle. "I'd better not let him pass us, just in case."

The driver behind began blowing his horn insistently. Bud still couldn't see through the snow-covered rear window. He stayed in the middle of the road and drove faster, overtaking the yellow car.

Dupuis shouted a sudden warning: "*Gare!*"

The yellow car ahead of them skidded to a broadside stop, blocking the way and trapping Bud and Dupuis between it and the car behind.

"Get out!" Bud yelled. "We're sitting ducks if—"

A gun cracked behind them.

Bud plunged out of the car and off the road into the snowdrift. He clawed and scrambled through. The gun fired behind him again; bark flew from a tree ahead. He flung himself behind some brush and dug deeper into the snow.

For a moment there was silence, except for muffled sounds from the city below. Then there were voices up on the road. Bud couldn't make out the words, but they sounded angry. One of the speakers was protesting. Another shot. Then a car door was slammed shut. The sound of the engine ceased, resumed, ceased, resumed as the car was turned around on the narrow road. Then the sound disappeared down the mountain.

Bud climbed back onto the road. Peewee came from the other side. They went to the body of the man sprawled in the snow beside the yellow car. He was dead.

It was the Marshal defenseman who had thrown the game to the Battlers.

"More thin ice," Bud muttered.

He and Dupuis, returning to their car to go for the police, found the gun on the front seat.

"Very thin ice," Peewee said, "for us."

10
Attack Zone

THE MONTREAL POLICE held Bud and Dupuis on suspicion of murder. Gleason ordered them not to say anything about *anything,* until his lawyer could fly up from Boise.

Early the next morning, with the lawyer present, the questioning started, and it lasted through the whole day. Bud and Dupuis refused to be deked from their original, truthful version of what had happened. Exactly twenty-four hours after their arrest, the two teammates were released without charge—on condition that they remain available for further questioning.

"You are free to go, gentlemen," Gleason said in a sarcastic imitation of the police detective, "but do not leave Montreal." He snorted. "Great. Just great. My two most important players grounded. For who knows *how* long!"

Dupuis grinned sheepishly. "At least we are not in jail."

"Not yet," Bud added with a frown. "What do we do now?"

"You sit and you wait," Gleason said. "The rest of the team has another game this week and one more on the road after that. I don't know how long you'll have to stay here in Montreal. You impressed the police with the way you refused to be shaken from your story. You weren't belligerent or evasive, as they expected you to be. And you displayed an understanding of their position. That made them pay more attention to what they found out on their own about the Marshal player.

"He'd never been in any trouble before, but he'd become vulnerable in recent months. Like Chuck, he'd had some staggering family medical expenses."

Gleason shook his head when he saw Bud and

Dupuis scowling. "I still don't think it's Chuck on our club, unless there's something we haven't uncovered."

"What about Ed Halloway, Mark Strickland's uncle?" Bud asked.

"No trace of him so far. Either he's got a disguise we haven't penetrated or he's hiding out."

"But the bets," Dupuis pointed out. "Who collected the money that was lost on the game here in Montreal?"

"The police looked into that at my suggestion," Gleason explained. "There was some small betting between private parties, and the police are convinced that's all it was. I don't think whoever's been fixing our games was interested in that angle on this particular game."

Bud squinted. "Are you suggesting he, or they, just wanted to get us back on a winning streak and then—"

Gleason cut in. "And then make a big killing at our Boise home game."

Dupuis looked doubtful.

"They must know now we will be watching. Do you think they would dare, in Boise, to—"

"If it were me," said Gleason, "I'd know that I'd either have to quit completely or try for one last big take before the lid is down for good. Our next game in Boise will be the last chance for it."

Bud shook his head. "It doesn't make sense. Not with all this in the open now."

"But it's *not* in the open," Gleason corrected him. "The police have given out a story that the Montreal player was killed in an attempted hold-up on the Mont Royale road. They're playing along so as not to scare the murderer to cover. Helping us solve our problem will uncover him for them. So we'll keep quiet and let them set up a fix in Boise. Then we'll trap them and solve two crimes at once."

"Three," Bud said grimly. "My dad's death, too."

Bud and Dupuis rejoined the club in Boise ten days later. The Montreal police had no further need for them in their investigation into the death of the Marshal player.

Greetings to Bud and Dupuis from their teammates were cool. "They know what other people don't," Tierney explained. "The sportswriters were told that Dupuis was out with his injury and that you, Bud, got the flu in Canada. I don't think they believed a word of it, but that's what they printed. However, the members of the club know that you were involved in the murder investigation."

"And," Bud said, "they also know that we had nothing to do with it. The police cleared us completely."

Tierney shook his head. "There's a rumor going around the club that Gleason somehow got you off."

Dupuis scowled. "Do they think he used magic? Bud and I spent ten days answering—"

"Wait a minute, Peewee," Bud interrupted. "Gleason probably started that rumor himself, to keep the spotlight on me. Now it's more important than ever that we don't scare away the fixer. We may never get another chance to trap him."

"*Oui.* But if we don't, the spotlight will still be shining on you, *mon ami.*"

Sportswriters had a lot of questions for Bud on Saturday morning. A lot of them were in Boise from out of town to cover the game with the Regina Regals. One writer persisted in suggesting that Bud's case of "flu" on the road was really a suspension.

"Hot air," Sid Seidler interposed. "How the

devil can you call it suspension? Look at Bud's standing in the tally of goals and assists. If you can't find anything better to write about in sports, you'd better go back to doing obituaries."

"Thanks, Sid," Bud said later.

"Keep your cool," Seidler said. "Where's Dupuis?"

"Skipped practice this morning," Bud replied. "Dropped me here, then went over to St. Al's. Doc Taylor wanted the hospital staff to double-check him and make sure the shoulder is okay for tonight's game." Bud saw his bantams arriving. "See you around, Sid."

Mrs. Strickland's hair looked as brassy as ever. Bud was surprised to see the Stricklands, after that phone call from Mark's father.

Strickland beckoned Bud to one side. "I'm sorry about my attitude the last time we spoke. If I'd known why you were asking—"

"You know now?" Bud asked tensely.

"I've had a lot of visitors," Strickland said, wincing. "Police; private investigators; your club owner, Gleason. It was embarrassing at first, but they've been very discreet." He paused and took a deep breath. "I should have known better than to get into gambling . . . betting on games. But because of my interest in the game, through Mark and my brother-in-law. . . .

"Well," Strickland continued, "I finally gathered from all the interrogation that Ed, my brother-in-law, was playing me for a sucker. He knew certain games were fixed, though he didn't tell me. He talked me into making that last big bet, which would have been lost if you hadn't tied the score."

Strickland looked around before he spoke again. "So I'm cooperating. I'm ready to place a large bet, with marked money, on tonight's game —if he shows up."

"You don't know where he is?" Bud asked.

"I wish I did. My wife and I aren't supposed to mention this to anyone, but I wanted you to know. I didn't think that, if you had any bad feelings toward me because of that phone call, you'd take them out on Mark—"

"Not at all, Mr. Strickland. Not even if you hadn't told me this. Thanks for telling me."

Bud blew his whistle for the start of the bantams' practice. It was good to know that the trap was set. But if Ed Halloway *was* caught and refused to talk, then the club would still be clouded with lingering suspicions. There was a traitor somewhere among them. That player would have to be tabbed tonight, before it was too late.

Dupuis and Bud were changing into their gear when Chuck arrived at the rink that evening.

"How's he doing?" Rod Stevens asked.

"Okay," Chuck sighed.

"Hospital again?" Art Schoen inquired. "Your father?"

Chuck nodded. From somewhere in the dressing room came a loud whisper. "Why always just before a big home game?"

Bud saw Chuck's hands clench. "Here we go again," he muttered to Dupuis.

But Chuck relaxed his hands and turned to the coach. "Any messages come for me, I don't want to know about them until *after* the game."

Tierney studied him. "That depends on what the message is . . . and how you tend goal. Okay, you're starting."

Bud saw expressions which conveyed that the coach's decision was not liked. It was not a good sign.

During the pregame warm-up, Bud spotted the Stricklands in the stands. Mark's uncle, Ed Halloway, was not with them. Bud returned

Mark's wave and glanced at Strickland, who shook his head slightly. Bud wondered if the trap had been discovered and was being avoided.

On the way to the dressing room, he saw Gleason in the corridor and paused beside him. "Any news?" he asked, his voice low.

Gleason shrugged. "There's been some heavy betting, but we haven't found Halloway yet. We've got people placing bets—"

"I know. Strickland told me." Bud frowned. "Do you suppose he's playing double agent . . . that he tipped off Halloway?"

"I doubt it, but it's a possibility. What about the game tonight?"

"Looks almost hopeless. We're still split apart. We're playing right into the hands of the fixer."

Lou Huff got the opening draw. The Battlers moved the puck toward the blue line and the attack zone, but their play lacked coordination. The Regals stole the puck and took the action toward the other blue line, then over into the Battler defense zone.

Dupuis closed in on the stickhandling Regal forward. Peewee was favoring the shoulder that had been separated; his shoulder check failed.

There were boos from the stands as the forward flipped the puck toward the goal. Chuck dove out from the crease to meet it. He tossed it behind the red line.

Rod Stevens sped around in back of the net and brought the puck out. He shot for the sideboards. The puck whizzed past Dupuis and the Regal forward and caromed from the boards to Bud. Taking it over the broken red line in neutral ice, Bud angled the puck over the blue.

Lou Huff took it on his stick just across the blue line, timing his charge perfectly, but the Regal center poke checked it away from him almost as soon as he received it. The attack went back toward the Battler goal. Chuck made another save, then another. Chuck's goaltending revived some fire in the Battler club. They began to coordinate. At 15:02 they scored!

Then Art Schoen took three strides, one too many, as he shoulder checked a Regal. The referee gave him two minutes for charging. Tierney sent in his penalty killers.

The Regals launched a power play. A Battler defenseman fell and was struck in the head by a stick. Blood trickled down into his eyes, blinding him. Play wasn't stopped for an injured

player until his team had possession of the puck. Bud shouted for the rest of the Battlers to close ranks. There wasn't a chance to get the puck and ice it or smother it to halt the play.

Half-blinded, the defenseman snagged his skate against another player's and went down again. A Regal stick flipped the puck over him and into the net.

Tie score.

The Regal goal ended Art Schoen's penalty. A substitute went in for the injured player. The Battlers were back to full strength, but neither team scored again before the period ended.

On the way to the dressing room, Tierney walked down the rubber mat beside Bud.

"Tex spoke to me at the bench. No Halloway yet. If the score stays tied—"

"They've *got* to make the fix happen," Bud said.

"Play to win. That'll force their hand. And let's hope we can spot it in time to stop it."

During the intermission, Bud tried once again to sort out all the doubts and suspicions he had developed during past games. He had a feeling that there was a pattern, but it was vague and fuzzy. He couldn't get it into focus.

Bud's mind was still spinning at the opening face-off, and he missed the pass from Lou Huff.

The fans booed, and they booed louder when the Regal defenseman slapped the puck from far back in neutral ice. Chuck flung himself into its path. It whacked him hard and bounced away. A Regal stick swept it into the goal as easily as sweeping out the kitchen.

Regals 2, Battlers 1.

If it continued like this, there would be no need for a fixed game. Bud glanced grimly at Dupuis, whose return glance reflected the same concern.

The Regal center got the puck at face-off. He took it over the blue line, then passed to his forward. Dupuis, no longer favoring his shoulder, gave a check that made the fans gasp. He took the puck into neutral ice, kept it, then took it across the broken red line.

"*Allons-y!*" he shouted, shooting from the blue line. In an instant, the puck was rebounding from the goalie, who was himself dazed by his save. A Regal defense swooped in to get the puck out of the crease.

The Regina club took the puck back to neutral ice, where Lou Huff dug it out with a poke check. The Battler forward line went into the attack zone, lost the puck, got it back in a wild scramble, and finally netted it at 12:05.

The score was still tied, 2–2, when the second period ended.

Gleason was in the corridor outside the dressing room. He motioned Tierney, Bud, and Dupuis aside.

"We've got Halloway. The police have him in my office now. He won't talk; claims he doesn't know any of our players personally."

"That's a big help," growled Tierney, glancing toward the dressing room. "A tie score, and we still don't know who—"

"I have a suggestion," Dupuis interrupted. "Have the police, with him in their custody, here in the corridor when we come out for next period." Peewee pointed to Gleason, Tierney, Bud, and himself. "We will watch faces; so will police. The guilty one will betray himself when he sees Halloway."

"We hope," said Tierney. "And if he doesn't—"

"It will mean either of two things," Bud said. "Either he's good at keeping himself deadpan, or Halloway is telling the truth."

"And that," Gleason said through his teeth, "could only mean that someone else has been making the contact for the fixes. Someone we—"

He broke off as the dressing room door opened. An assistant trainer peered through the doorway. "Al," he called to the coach, "we've been wondering where you were. Doc Taylor's having trouble with Bates. He wants to play if you need him this period, but Doc thinks—"

"I'll talk to him," Tierney said. The group in the corridor broke up.

Bud, Tierney, and Dupuis were first out the door when the warning buzzer sounded. The police, apparently having just made an arrest, were bringing Halloway down the corridor against the tide of Battler players. Bud, Dupuis, and the coach paused to turn and watch the police and their prisoner, but they were really looking at teammates' faces. No one showed any sign of surprise or any unusual reaction other than natural curiosity.

One alternate player asked Gleason what it was all about. Gleason shrugged, waited until they were alone, then moved to Tierney and Bud.

"Guess it's the hard way: on the ice."

The Regal center got the puck on the opening face-off of the third period.

"Peewee!" Bud shouted warningly.

Dupuis moved over, ready to skate back and help Chuck defend the goal. The Battlers got the rubber and took it down to the attack zone; the Regals made a stand and prevented a goal. Then the puck went toward the Battler goal.

Rod Stevens attempted a hip check, but the Regal forward roughed him, giving him an elbow in the face. Rod closed in, pulling off his gloves. They mixed it up.

It took the referee, a linesman, and other players to separate them. Both went to the penalty bench and sat at opposite ends.

The puck went back and forth on the rink, both teams alternately attacking, then defending. Ten minutes went by. Neither side scored. Bud felt incredible tension. If there was going to be an attempt at a fix to let the Regals win, it would have to be soon.

Trouble came where Bud least expected it. The Regals had the puck and were attacking, when, in the midst of the melee, the referee's whistle blasted. He pointed at Dupuis and signaled tripping. The fans protested loudly.

Bud, as team captain, spoke to the official. "It wasn't intentional—"

"I can't read a player's mind," the referee retorted. "I only call what I see."

He skated into the referee's crease and told the timekeeper that Dupuis was penalized for two minutes.

Bud groaned. One man short—of all times! Dupuis looked apologetic, and Bud gave him a grim smile. Tierney called in Art and Lou and replaced them with two penalty killers; the Regal bench replaced their defensemen with forwards. It was going to be a long two minutes.

The Battlers stood off a blazing attack on their goal for thirty seconds. Suddenly the whistle blasted again. The referee pointed at Rod Stevens and signaled cross-checking. Howls and boos came from the stands.

Bud approached the ref again. "I didn't see—"

"Of course not, captain. You were at the other side of the crease. But I was there. I saw it and called it."

Bud stood in the referee's way, and the man gave him a hard look. "Now, stop arguing, or I'll slap you with a ten-minute misconduct."

He skated around Bud toward the halfcircle

crease where the penalty timekeeper sat.

The fans were on their feet, shouting, booing, throwing things on the ice. There was a hail of wadded paper, soft drink containers, cups filled with crushed ice, even seat cushions.

Bud stood rooted, staring toward the penalty box. Art Schoen skated up to him.

"It's a tough one to take, Bud, but it was a fair call on Rod. It was cross-checking. I'd have called it that way myself."

Bud kept his eyes on the penalty box. "Okay, maybe it was a fair call. But could Rod have cross-checked unintentionally?"

Art snorted. "How can you cross-check unintentionally? You have to—" He stopped. "Bud, are you saying—"

"You just confirmed it for me, Art. That was a deliberate penalty. Rod's our man!"

The fans were still booing and throwing things. The ice was littered with junk. Resumption of play was impossible. The officials called for a ten-minute recess, to cool off the spectators and clear the ice.

Players from both teams were milling around the rink. Bud wove between his teammates and opposing players toward the penalty box. Dupuis

was there; Rod Stevens was not! Glancing quickly around, Bud saw him—at the opposite side of
the rink, opening the gate that led off the ice
and to the dressing room. No one else seemed to
notice that he was leaving.

"Stevens!" Bud lunged into a fast drive across
the rink. "Peewee! Stop him!"

Rod Stevens heard the shout, turned, saw Bud
coming. He threw his stick into Bud's path and
hurried through the gate. Bud swerved to avoid
the stick, couldn't slow in time, and slammed
hard into the boards.

Dupuis, close behind, hoisted Bud upright
with a handful of jersey, and together they stumbled down the rubber-matted corridor toward
the dressing room. The dressing room door was
locked from the inside, but Dupuis opened it
with a shoulder check. Then he charged at
Stevens.

"Wait, Peewee!" Bud shouted.

"Hey! What the—" Tierney called from behind them.

"What's going on here? Stop it!" Gleason bellowed above the sudden commotion in the dressing room as he and several players poured in
through the broken door.

Dupuis was holding Rod Stevens in a massive bear hug.

"Isn't it a little early to be changing clothes, Rod?" Bud asked, breathing heavily. "The game isn't over yet."

"Put him down," Gleason ordered Dupuis. Peewee dumped Rod onto the bench. "Somebody get the police," Gleason said over his shoulder, then turned to stare icily at Rod. "Okay, start talking. Make it good!"

Gleason, Tierney, and the members of the team formed a tight, hard circle around Rod Stevens. For a moment he looked from face to face; then he lowered his gaze and spoke slowly.

"Two years ago, after a game, I . . . I ran over an old man. It was dark; he was drunk. He just walked right in front of my car. I stopped to help him, but he was dead. And . . . and there weren't any witnesses. I mean, I thought at the time that there weren't any witnesses."

Two uniformed policemen and a plainclothes detective had joined the circle of listeners.

"So I left him there," Rod went on. "Later, I got a phone call. Somebody who had seen the whole thing."

"And," said Bud, "he's used it to twist your

arm ever since. Forced you to throw games—by handicapping us with penalties, or letting the offense get by you with the puck, or screening Chuck's view of the offense. . . ."

"And that rigged goalie's stick," Lou Huff added. "You were real palsy-walsy with Chuck, always waiting at the hospital with him while his dad—"

"Yeah, it fits," Gleason interrupted. "Chuck, I got a message from the hospital right after the game started. Your dad's okay. He began wondering why he always had another attack on the night of an important game. He mentioned it to his doctor, and they checked it out. The attacks were triggered by something in his food."

"You!" Chuck blazed at Rod. "You're always at our house, snacking in our kitchen, eating meals with us—" Before anyone could react, Chuck had his hands around Rod's neck. Several teammates pulled him back and restrained him.

"And what about *my* father?" Bud demanded. "Did you—"

"No! No, really, Bud. I didn't touch him. He was onto us . . . followed me up to Table Rock that night. I was meeting my . . . my partner there. Your father caught me. Told me he knew everything, that he was going to the police. My partner sneaked up behind him and hit him, knocked him unconscious. Then he told me to leave; he said he'd take care of your dad. But I didn't know he would—"

"Put my father back in his car and roll it off the edge," Bud finished for him. "With a sackful of money under his coat for effect. Who is it?" Bud shouted. "Who?"

The warning buzzer sounded in the dressing room. The game would resume in three minutes. There were nervous, anxious mutterings among the players.

"Wait a minute," Bud exclaimed. "I know who it is! I should have known from the start. It's somebody with access to all the players, somebody well liked and trusted by them. A sharp dresser . . . a fast talker—"

"Sid Seidler!" Gleason snapped.

"Sid Seidler." Rod said it quietly, matter-of-factly.

The police turned hurriedly to leave, but Tierney stopped them. "Hold on. Seidler's not going anywhere. He's waiting out there for us to lose the game, so he can collect." Tierney turned to his team. "And I want him to see us win this one—win in spite of him. We'll win this game for Bud's father. Now, get out there and melt that ice!"

"*Allons-y!*" Dupuis shouted.

"I just can't believe it." Sid Seidler, notebook in hand, was at the gate leading off the ice, surrounded by breathless Battlers. "I can't believe you won that game, and with two men in the box!"

Jubilant Battlers fans were emptying from the stands, still applauding and cheering their team's amazing come-from-behind victory.

"Tierney must have given you some talk during that recess," Seidler went on. "I've never seen such an exciting eight minutes of hockey in my life. I just can't *believe* you won that game."

"I'll bet you can't," Bud said with an ironic grin. Over Seidler's shoulder, he could see the police closing in. "Well, Sid, the pen may be mightier than the sword, but sometimes the hockey stick is mightier than the pen!"

Seidler chuckled. "I'll remember that for my column, Bud. That's pretty good. Maybe—"

Seidler stopped talking as two policemen, one on either side, took hold of his arms. His friendly expression turned suddenly cold.

Bud nodded. "I'm glad you liked it, Sid. You can write it up for the prison newspaper. Don't forget to give some credit to Ed Halloway and Rod Stevens, too."

Seidler made no reply. The police led him away.

The dressing room was unusually quiet . . . especially considering the team's miraculous victory. No one knew quite how to react to everything that had taken place during the game. The players undressed slowly, in silence.

Finally, Bud spoke up, loudly enough for all to hear. "Peewee, I'll always remember that expression on Seidler's face. For once the great sportswriter was at a loss for words. He had nothing to say."

There were approving murmurs from Bud's teammates.

"Well, I have something to say," Tierney bellowed. All eyes turned toward him. "You guys finally played some pretty good hockey out there. I'm proud of you. But don't let victory go to your heads, you clowns. And don't forget practice tomorrow morning—eight o'clock sharp!"

Moans and groans from the team members quickly dissolved into laughter and cheering.

"*Magnifique!*" said Dupuis.

"*Oui!*" Bud said. "*Oui!*"

Whitman CLASSICS and ANTHOLOGIES

Black Beauty

Little Women

Heidi

Heidi Grows Up

Tom Sawyer

Huckleberry Finn

The Call of the Wild

Treasure Island

Alice in Wonderland

The Wonderful Wizard of Oz

Famous Fairy Tales

Algonquin: The Story of a Great Dog

Tales of Poe

SHORT STORY COLLECTIONS

A Batch of the Best (Stories for Girls)

Like It Is (Stories for Girls)

Shudders

Golden Prize

That's Our Cleo! *(New)*

Way Out *(New)*

Whitman NOVELS FOR GIRLS

Spirit Town

Gypsy From Nowhere

The Family Name

True to You

Practically Twins

Make-Believe Daughter

The Silver Seven

Bicycles North! *(New)*

WHITMAN ®

Whitman ADVENTURE and MYSTERY Books

THE TRIXIE BELDEN SERIES
16 Exciting Titles

MEG MYSTERIES
The Disappearing Diamonds
The Secret of the Witch's Stairway
The Treasure Nobody Saw
The Ghost of Hidden Springs
The Mystery of the Black-Magic Cave
Mystery in Williamsburg

DONNA PARKER
Takes a Giant Step
On Her Own
Mystery at Arawak
Special Agent

KIM ALDRICH MYSTERIES
Miscalculated Risk
Silent Partner
The Deep Six *(New)*
The Long Shot *(New)*

TELEVISION FAVORITES
Lassie
  Lost in the Snow
  Trouble at Panter's Lake
The Mod Squad
Hawaii Five-O
Family Affair

SPORTS AND ADVENTURE STORIES
Throw the Long Bomb! (Football)
Basket Fever (Basketball)
Cellar Team (Baseball)
Drag Strip Danger (Racing)
Divers Down! (Undersea Adventure)

TEE-BO, THE TALKING DOG
2 Titles in This Rollicking New Series

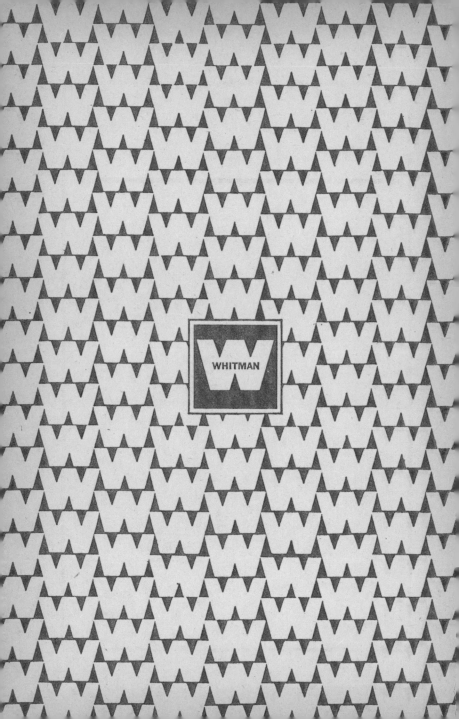